CYNTHIA HICKEY

Wedding Day Cat Burglar
(A Tail-Waggin' Mystery)
By Cynthia Hickey

To animal and mystery lovers everywhere.

Chapter One

A gray cat peeked at me from under one of the chairs set up for Heather's wedding, then turned its attention to batting the huge white bow taped to the chair arm. The dangers of an outdoor wedding. "Come out of there, you rascal." I hiked up my yellow bridesmaid dress and lowered to my knees. Heather would kill me if I got dirty.

"Got 'cha!" I gripped the cat behind the neck, resulting in a nasty scratch for my effort. "You beast." I dropped the feline, which streaked into the reception hall. Let it be someone else's problem. I straightened the bow and headed for the room at the back of the hall where my best friend was getting ready for her wedding.

"Everything's good for the ceremony," I said, entering the room. The worry on Heather's face stopped me in my tracks. "What's wrong?"

"What if this marriage is no better than my first?" She raised tear-filled eyes.

"David is nothing like your first husband." I sat

on a padded bench next to her.

"I thought Bobby was a good man, too, when I married him."

"Well, I think David is the best. That counts for something. Dry your eyes before you ruin your makeup." I gave her a one-armed hug. "You look gorgeous, by the way. It's a beautiful day; the sun has cast diamonds across the surface of the lake. We'd best finish here if you want to make the ceremony by sunset."

"You're right. I'm being silly. Help me with my veil." She stood so I could insert the comb holding the short veil into the bun on her head.

"Where did I put my earrings?" She turned and searched the counter. "They go with my necklace. David bought me these as a wedding gift." She touched the diamonds at her throat.

"They're here somewhere. Wear mine." I removed my studs and dropped them into her hand. "It's more important that you're complete than me." Smiling, I opened the door to peek out. "Guests are arriving."

Mom and Shar, both wearing dresses that matched the one I wore, hurried into the room. My mother hadn't stopped grinning since Heather asked her to be a bridesmaid.

"I feel like a young girl again." She twirled, sending the hem of the dress dancing around her knees.

"There's a cat running wild in the reception hall." Shar smoothed her dress. "I tried to catch it, but it hissed at me."

"I'm already wearing battle wounds." I showed

them my scratch, then headed to the bathroom to clean it. When I finished, Heather stood in the doorway, her arm linked with the arm of my father, who would give her hand to David's.

"Someday, this will be me and you." He smiled.

Yes, someday, when I let go of my foolish notion that marriage meant losing one's independence. Brad, my fiancé, didn't try to stifle my dreams or even keep me from sticking my nose where it didn't belong. The fact we hadn't set a date rested solely on my shoulders.

I pasted a smile to my lips, grabbed my bouquet from Shar, and took my place in line as the music started to play. As I moved toward the front of the white carpet runner, my gaze settled on Brad. I'd seen him dressed up before, but somehow today in his tuxedo, he'd never been more handsome.

He put his hand over his heart and winked.

Mercy, that man did things to my blood pressure.

Heather handed me her bouquet and faced her groom as the sun started to settle over the lake. Instead of diamonds, the water now sported a river of gold. The perfect backdrop for a special day.

After the ceremony and wedding photos, I headed to the reception hall to make sure the wedding table had been prepared to my standards. Crystal flutes, candles, and flowers set a romantic tone on each table. Guests partook of *hors d'oeuvre before the meal was served. A DJ played soothing music from a corner of the room. Everything was set.*

A gray streak speeding past had me gritting my

teeth. That darn stray cat had a shrimp in its mouth.

"One of yours?" McIlroy grinned over the rim of a wineglass.

"No. It would be better behaved." I chuckled. "Beautiful ceremony, wasn't it?"

"Yep. Want to know what's even more beautiful? The fact you haven't almost gotten anyone killed in five months."

"Shar is chomping at the bit." Since she, myself, and my mother called ourselves The Waterfall Sleuths—Shar's idea, not mine—she grew irritable without a dangerous crime to solve. "Excuse me." I wanted to refresh my lipstick before giving the toast.

In the ladies' room, a woman opened every stall, glanced around, then hurried to the hole in the counter for the trashcan. "It has to be here."

"Can I help you?"

"I set my ruby ring on the counter before using the restroom, then realized I'd set it down after washing cocktail sauce off my hands, and now it's gone." She rubbed her temple. "Whoever I heard come in must have taken it."

"Are you sure?" I helped her look until I had no more time to spare. "I'm so sorry, but I need to go." A quick smear of lipstick and I was off.

At the wedding party table, I clinked my butter knife against my flute to grab everyone's attention. The noise subsided, and I raised my glass of champagne. "I think everyone here knows me, but I'm Trinity Ashford, Heather Johnson's best friend." It would take some getting used to saying her new name. "We've been friends since kindergarten and taken part in every important event of each other's life. I can't begin to explain how lucky David is to have her as his wife."

I cleared my throat and blinked away tears. "She's a super woman, even if she doesn't want to be a Waterfall Sleuth. Let's raise our glasses to this couple who are beautiful inside and out."

Cheers rose as flutes lifted high. I gazed up into Brad's face. I was ready to set our own wedding date. It had nothing to do with the romance of the moment. Why put off what I deeply longed for?

After a meal of steak and baked potato, I took my place on the dance floor as the dancing started. After the specialty ones, I stood ready to collect the money offered to dance with the bride or groom.

Robbie stood next to his mommy, staring up at her with big eyes. "Dance, Mommy?"

"Of course." Heather took his hands in hers and twirled him around the floor while I looked for his grandparents. Heather's ex-husband's parents would watch her son Robbie when she and David went to Hawaii for their honeymoon. After a couple of spins, she returned her son to my side.

"I'm special," Robbie said, standing next to me in a tuxedo identical to the one David wore.

"Yes, you are." I smiled down at him.

"I have a new daddy."

"Oh." I smiled. "That *is* special."

He nodded. "I like him, but not him dancing with my mommy." He marched to squeeze between them as those watching laughed.

David hefted him up with one arm, turning the dance for two into one for three. My smile widened.

A special family indeed.

Brad swept me onto the dance floor as the wedding party was called to join the bride and groom. "Have I told you how beautiful you are?"

"Not today."

"I'm sorry for that. You're the prettiest gal here." He pulled me close.

"Don't let the bride hear you."

"What happened to your earrings?" His breath tickled my neck.

"Heather misplaced hers, so I lent her mine." I opened my mouth to let him know I wanted to set a date when I spotted the cat on the buffet table nibbling at a filet mignon. "That's it!" I stepped away from Brad and hurried to the table. Since the cat was intent on its meal, it didn't see me coming. I tossed a napkin over its head and snatched the thief off the table.

"Here." Brad opened a nearby door which led to a small supply closet. "This ought to hold the rascal."

I set the cat inside the closet and stepped back so Brad could shut the door before the little beast could escape. Who did he belong to? None of the servers seemed upset to see him; none of the guests seemed concerned about the cat. Most watched his antics with amusement. Which meant he was most likely a stray, and I'd need to contact animal control who would be closed at this time of the night.

"Let's finish our dance." Brad took my hand and led me to the dance floor as another slow song began to play.

Once again, I started to let him know I'd made

my decision when one of the servers headed for the closet. "Don't open that door!" I raced in her direction.

Too late. She opened the closet, pulled out a broom, and the gray cat shot out and darted under the buffet table.

This would be quite comical under different circumstances, but I didn't want anything to ruin Heather's evening. Especially a rowdy animal.

I rushed to the table and dropped to my knees. Lifting the tablecloth that brushed the floor, I came face-to-face with a dead guy. I knew he was dead because a steak knife protruded from his chest, and he stared at me with lifeless eyes.

Chapter Two

The night was ruined after all. I scooted backwards, letting the edge of the tablecloth fall into place, then went in search of McIlroy.

He sat sipping another glass of wine next to Shar. "Hey, Trinity."

"We have a problem." I whispered in his ear about the dead guy.

He exhaled long and slow. "Go close the doors. No one is leaving here anytime soon." He rose to his feet and took the microphone from the DJ. "Folks, my apologies, but there's been a murder, and no one leaves until they've been cleared." He handed the mic back to the wide-eyed DJ, then strode to the table, his shoes slapping the floor in a steady beat—the only sound in the now quiet room. Until Heather wailed, anyway.

Gathering her in his arms, David shot me a glare. What? It wasn't my fault. I stepped outside and ushered everyone to the patio inside, then closed the double doors behind me.

Rather than head back to their tables, everyone crowded around the buffet table. McIlroy's face darkened as he called for backup. "Because I've had a few glasses of wine and need the help." If he could have slammed his cell phone down, he would have.

I had no idea who would come help him. Other than McIlroy, our small-town police force seemed to have a revolving door with officers coming and leaving Waterfall on a consistent basis.

"Return to your tables, please," McIlroy said. "I'll start calling you over one at a time. After you've been questioned, you'll be free to go home."

Even when help arrived, it would take all night. McIlroy started with the servers.

I headed to the table where my parents sat, Brad at my side.

"Who is it?" Mom asked.

"Does Alex know anything?" Shar arched a brow.

"Don't know, and I doubt it." I cast a glance at the wedding table where Heather and David now sat alone. "They blame me."

"No, they don't." Brad put an arm around me.

"Sure. Go ask them." I gave him a push.

"Are you serious?"

I nodded.

He went to the front of their table, said something, and returned. "They kind of do. Heather said trouble follows you like a puppy after a chew toy."

"That isn't my fault." It was a gift I'd rather not have, this tendency for trouble. For getting involved

WEDDING DAY CAT BURGLAR

in mysteries. It had been a peaceful five months. I leaned my elbow on the table and rested my chin in my hand.

"That isn't proper posture, dear." Mom tapped my arm.

"I don't care." I glanced at the buffet table. McIlroy had left the cloth down to hide the poor dead man. Since he'd worn a suit, I felt safe in saying the departed was a guest. So, why hadn't anyone revealed his identity?

I tapped my foot under the table, itching to start asking questions of my own. When I couldn't contain my jitters any longer, I jumped up and marched to the wedding table. "I'm sorry. I tried to make your wedding special, but I cannot control the evil doings of man or woman."

Heather blinked like an owl, her mascara smeared. "I know that. But why does this always happen when you're around?"

"It's a gift." I shrugged, eliciting a smile from her. "Do you know the man?"

"I couldn't see him from here." She shrank back against David.

"If one of you could take a look, it would be a big help to McIlroy."

"I'll go." David stood and headed to the table. Ignoring McIlroy's protests, he lifted the tablecloth and stumbled backward.

I bolted to my feet and rushed to hear what he said to the detective. "You know him?"

"He's my boss, Walter Jennings."

"Any idea why someone wants your boss dead?" McIlroy tilted his head.

"None. He's...was...a good boss."

"Family?"

"Divorced. Grown children." David rubbed his hands roughly down his face. "Excuse me. I'd like to go back to my bride." He whirled and rushed away.

"At least you know who he is now," I said.

"I knew from the wallet in his pocket. What I didn't know was his connection to David. Finally." He glanced around me as two uniformed officers approached. He introduced them as Officer Rice and Officer Snowe. The two rookies didn't look old enough to be out of high school. He filled them in on what he knew.

Officer Snowe raised a brow in my direction, her pretty face devoid of makeup. "Should you be speaking in front of a civilian and potential suspect?"

I frowned. "I'm not a suspect. I found the body while chasing a cat."

"Where's the cat now?" I didn't think her brow could lift any higher, but it did.

"No idea. Probably ran outside before I could close the doors." Either way, I no longer cared about the feline.

"Take it easy on Miss Ashford, Officer." McIlroy motioned to an empty table. "She's been a lot of help in past cases. She's intuitive. Each of you take a table and start motioning folks over so we can finish this. Since you're here, Trinity, have a seat."

I'd hoped he would be the one questioning me, but instead I got the Ice Queen. I plopped into a chair and crossed my arms. "I'm Trinity Ashford, best friend of the bride, and owner of Tail Waggin', a pet store and daycare."

"You've done this before?" She started writing on a notepad.

"Yep."

"Start with the cat."

"Is it a suspect, too?"

She lifted her stony gaze from the tablet. "I'm asking the questions."

I told her everything I knew about the cat. "Here's a juicy tidbit for you." I leaned my elbows on the table. "The bride's set of earrings went missing. See that woman in the floral dress? She's missing a ruby ring."

"We're investigating a murder, Miss Ashford, not theft."

"The two could be connected." I tapped my temple. "Intuitive, remember?"

"Are you going to be a problem?"

Probably. I grinned and shrugged.

"You're finished. Send over someone else from your table."

I sent Brad. "Careful. She's prickly."

"I can handle prickly women." He kissed my cheek.

Of course, he could. She'd probably be putty in his hands. Most women were once he turned his gorgeous eyes on them. I resumed my seat.

"I don't think Officer Snowe and I are going to be friends," I told the others.

"Why would you want to be?" Shar frowned. "You have me and Heather. You don't need any more friends. We're going to be busy solving this case anyway."

"It's not a wise thing when one of the officers on the case thinks you're a suspect."

"Pshaw." She waved a dismissive hand. "Alex will be in charge. Those two will only do the grunt work. We need to find out all we know about the victim."

"He's David's boss. Name is Walter Jennings. Divorced with grown children. That's it." I brought up the missing jewelry items. "It's too much of a coincidence to think the two aren't related."

"I agree," Dad said. "What are the odds of two crimes happening at the same wedding?"

"You're right. She's prickly." Brad sat down and told Shar it was her turn.

"Well, she isn't going to rattle me." Head high, Shar strode toward Snowe. She returned five minutes later. "I do not like that woman. The officer didn't even care that Alex and I are an item. Had the nerve to tell me that if I interfere in the investigation, she'd have me arrested."

"Alex has been threatening that for months." I chuckled.

"Good luck, Anne. You're up." Shar took a sip of her wine.

Mom nodded, seemingly unrattled.

My head jerked around to hear laughter from the Ice Queen seconds after my mother sat across from her. I kept staring to make sure I hadn't imagined it. No, she laughed again.

"She isn't so bad," Mom said when she returned. "Your turn, Joe."

"What did you say to make her laugh?" I asked as Dad left.

"First, I told her I was your mother. She laughed and offered her condolences. Then, I told her that I worked for the police department but was one of the Waterfall Sleuths during my off hours. I'm not sure why, but that cracked her up the most. I don't think she believed me. Am I that old that I can't be taken seriously?" Her eyes widened.

"I doubt that's it." Surely, the officer had heard of the Waterfall Sleuths. We'd been mentioned in the local paper several times. "Since they're done with me, I'm going to start cleaning up. We're going to be here until early morning as it is."

The others agreed to help and boxed up decorations and handed out the floral centerpieces for people to take home. Someone ought to enjoy the flowers before they died. My gaze flicked back to the now cleared buffet table. Except for the tablecloth. That still gave the deceased his privacy.

Slowly, hour after hour, the reception hall emptied. The DJ had been questioned and released a long time ago. Since they had a plane to catch, Heather returned my earrings and left with David. Soon, only law enforcement and my family, Shar, and Brad stayed.

"What about the gifts?" Shar asked.

"Brad will take them to his place until Heather and David return. Then, we'll have a party and watch them open the gifts." I closed the last box, every inch of my body heavy with exhaustion. My poor dog, Sheba, must be itching to go outside.

My father and Brad carried everything to my

SUV. Two men from the morgue collected the body. With nothing left for us to do, we shuffled away. Since McIlroy hadn't finished, Brad offered to drop Shar off at her house.

"Can we just stay here tonight?" I asked when we reached my place. "I barely have the energy to take Sheba out."

"Go ahead and get ready for bed. I'll take the dog out." He tucked a wayward strand of hair away from my face. "It was a beautiful ceremony."

"And a reception not to be forgotten." I climbed the stairs to my apartment. Sheba bounded out the front door the second I opened it and joined Brad downstairs.

I took the pins out of my hair, removed my makeup, and sat on the sofa to wait for Brad. But I fell asleep and didn't wake up for eight hours. The crick in my neck brought a groan.

Brad slept in the recliner across from me, both cats curled up on his lap.

"What about Barney?" I asked. I'd forgotten all about his beagle.

"I had the concierge take him out," he mumbled. "I'm glad today is Sunday because I need a day to recuperate."

Me, too. I glanced at my phone, surprised to see a text from Shar. I opened it and read, "Jennings had a pair of diamond earrings in his jacket pocket."

Chapter Three

For a week, I heard nothing more about the murder or thefts. I still hadn't told Brad that I'd set a date. Instead, I sat here at the counter of Tail Waggin' and wondered what was wrong with me. I'd been in a funk since the wedding.

"I know what will cheer you up," Mom said.

"What?"

"Your father and I bought a pontoon boat. We're taking you and Brad out today, so close up shop. We're all taking a day off."

"I own a business, Mom. I can't take off willy-nilly."

She glanced around the shop. "You don't look busy to me. Besides, Shar is here."

"Sure, I'll hold down the fort." Shar came into the room and set some dog shampoo on the shelf. "I've some grooming to do so have to stay behind. Not that anyone asked me to go." Nose in the air, she stormed to the back of the shop.

"Next time," Mom called. "The pontoon isn't that big." She lowered her voice. "It's big enough,

17

but you need some cheering up. Grab your purse and Sheba. I've made us a picnic lunch. The men will be here any minute."

I locked the cats in the apartment. By the time Sheba and I stepped outside, Dad's truck had arrived, a twenty-foot pontoon boat pulling behind. Excitement started to grow. I could use a day on the lake.

Sheba and I climbed into the backseat of the truck with Brad. "Hello, sweetheart." He leaned over and kissed me. "What's wrong?"

"Just in a funk." I smiled. "But I'm better now." I really was. Seeing his face told me all I needed to know. He'd been so busy that week we hadn't spent much time together.

"Do you know how to drive that thing?" I asked Dad.

He glanced in the rearview mirror. "The man I bought it from took me for a quick run around the lake. Piece of cake."

Didn't fill me with assurance, but nothing would ruin this day. The rest of us climbed out of the truck as Dad backed up to the boat launch. "Let me know when to stop, Brad."

"Will do." Brad moved to where he could see. When Dad's rear tires hit the water and the pontoon floated, he unhooked the boat and yelled for Dad to pull forward. So far so good.

"How do we climb on?" I stared at the ladder with steps barely big enough for my toes. "How do we get the dogs on?"

"We lift them. Hold the rope." Brad tossed it to me.

I missed.

The boat started to pull away. I splashed into the water up to my waist and grabbed hold, the boat still straining to drift toward the trees on the other side of the lake. "Now what?"

"Pull it back." Brad joined me and took the rope. "It'll pull easy in the water." This time, he tossed the rope to Dad, then, grunting, hefted Sheba up and over. Once the mastiff was in, he turned to Honey, Mom's Corgi. "You're much lighter. The rest of you climb up. I'm already wet so I'll hold her still, then climb aboard."

"There has to be a better way." I climbed onboard.

"If I was docked somewhere, all we'd have to do was step in." Dad grinned and sat in the captain's chair. He started moving before I'd taken my seat.

I stumbled, fighting to regain my footing and fell onto a bench. "A little warning, please."

"Sorry." Out in the open water, Dad increased our speed.

I lifted my face to the breeze and smiled. A beautiful day to be on the water.

"Guess what I heard at work yesterday?" Mom waggled her eyebrows.

"What?" Please don't be anything that will ruin this day.

"There's a suspected jewel thief in town. A cat burglar. Someone who sneaks in and out of homes with nary a clue."

"I know what a cat burglar is. Let's not talk mysteries today." Why Waterfall? Our little town

19

sure saw more than its share of crime. Sure, we had people with money, but wouldn't a larger city offer more opportunities for those wanting to steal? Ugh. She'd diverted my mind away from the wind in my hair and the sun on my face.

"I thought we could pass the time by talking," she said.

"Sometimes doing absolutely nothing is the best thing." I closed my eyes and lifted my face again.

"Be that way, but I'm telling you the cat burglar was at the wedding. You did say some jewelry went missing."

I sighed and faced her. "Yes, I did. The police have found nothing. They haven't even come by to question me again."

"Because they know you didn't kill Mr. Jennings."

"How would they know that? Officer Snowe seemed like she'd have loved for me to be the culprit."

"I told her you didn't do it. How could you when you were always in plain sight waiting on the bride and groom? Besides, you're too small to have dragged the dead guy under that table."

I straightened. "He wasn't killed there?"

"Well, yes, but I doubt the fight for his life was under the table. More like beside it. They found the blood splatters, what was left of them anyway. The servers thought someone had spilled cocktail sauce and mopped it up."

I frowned. "It doesn't look the same at all." That meant Mr. Jennings had to have been killed during the ceremony and hidden under the buffet table.

"Not everyone is as experienced as we are, dear. Drink?" Mom opened the cooler by her feet and tossed me a diet soda.

"We'll have lunch here." Dad pulled into a small cove. "Brad, grab that tree over there. Make sure I don't bump it too hard."

"Do you think there are snakes up there? I'd like to get out and take a picture of that waterfall." Mom pointed.

Brad sprang to his feet and headed for the front. He started to put his hand on the tree trunk but jumped back.

The boat bumped the tree.

"Snake on the boat!" Brad started backpedaling.

Mom screamed and scrambled onto a folding metal table.

I shrieked and stood on the bench as Brad and the snake reached me. The snake stretched up, trying to get on my bench. I yelled and either kicked it or hit it. Couldn't really tell in my panicked state. Either way, it fell back to the floor and continued chasing Brad, finally taking shelter behind the ice chest.

Brad slapped the chest away and grabbed the boat anchor.

The snake coiled and opened its mouth.

"That's a cottonmouth." My heart beat in my throat. I grabbed the rod holding up the awning and contemplated a leap overboard. The sight of jagged rocks had me jumping and screaming on the bench instead.

Brad whacked at the snake with the anchor.

Sheba stuck her big head in the way, retreating

when I told her to move back. Honey decided to get involved and snapped at the snake.

"Sheba, Honey, get back!" I yelled.

Confused, they backed away, clearly wanting to help. We didn't need any snake bites, human or canine.

After several hits, the snake coiled around the anchor, unable to go anywhere.

"Someone hand me the pole you use to insert into the floor for the table." Brad held out his hand.

Mom handed it to me, then I handed it to him. Brad put the pole firmly on the snake's head, then pulled a pocketknife from his jeans and cut off its head. The disgusting thing's mouth still opened and closed.

"Ew. Throw it overboard!" My body trembled.

"Where is it? Where is it?" Mom crawled along the opposite bench.

"In the water." Brad tossed both head and body overboard.

"That sure was something." Dad lowered his feet from where he'd propped them on the dashboard. "Glad you didn't put a hole in my boat with that anchor."

"Brad, you are definitely the hero of the day." I sagged into my seat.

"Didn't have a choice. I guess I could have opened one of the doors. Maybe the snake would have returned to the lake, but I wasn't thinking straight."

"I'm bleeding." Mom plopped down next to me. "There's a medical kit under the bench I was on."

My hands shook so bad I could hardly open the

box. "I'm sorry. You'll have to tend to yourself."

"Let's eat." Dad instructed Brad to tie us to the tree.

"We can't eat here. I want to go out there. In the middle of the lake. Please." I widened my eyes. "Away from trees that drop snakes into boats."

"All right, daughter." Dad backed the pontoon boat out of the cove.

"That was exciting." Brad grinned.

"I'm surrounded by crazy people." I wrapped my arms around Sheba's neck. "You good girl, trying to help Brad fight that bad snake."

"It was only three feet long," Dad said. "Not an anaconda."

"I didn't see you trying to help." I glared.

"If it had bitten me, who would have driven the boat?"

I really was surrounded by crazy people.

"Here's your sandwich." Mom, sporting fresh gauze on her leg, handed me a ham and cheese. "Your hand is shaking so bad, try not to drop it. I only brought one each."

"Seriously? We could have been bitten, and you're worried about me dropping a sandwich?"

"It's over now. You'll laugh about it someday."

"Look." Brad pointed to the sky.

An American eagle swooped from the bright blue and snatched a fish from the water. With his meal dangling from its claws, he flew to a tree and proceeded to eat.

Dad cut the engine. We ate our sandwiches and enjoyed the view of the eagle also having lunch. Slowly, my heart rate returned to normal.

"I guess God answered my question about snakes," Mom said.

"Then sent us an eagle to enjoy." I smiled.

After we'd eaten, Dad took another spin around the lake before pulling up to the boat launch. "Now, that was a day we all needed," he said.

"Minus the snake." I studied the water before climbing from the boat, not wanting to step on one that might be swimming around.

Brad followed, helping the dogs down, then pulled the pontoon closer for Mom and Dad.

I napped against Brad's shoulder on the way home. Shar was just closing up for the day when we arrived.

She listened with wide eyes as I told her about our day. "I'm glad I wasn't invited, then. I'd have had a heart attack and been snake food."

"It wasn't big enough to eat you." Dad laughed and waved out the window as he and Mom drove away.

"Despite that particular adventure," I said, "it was a wonderful day."

"Let me stick with killers and thieves—the human kind of snakes." Shar hefted her purse on her shoulder. "Can't stand snakes. See you tomorrow. Oh, someone dropped off a litter of Pomeranians for you to sell."

"Are you coming?" I glanced back, reaching for the door.

"I'll be by in a bit," Brad said. "I have some paperwork to do. Wanna watch a movie later? *Anaconda, Snakes on a Plane*?"

"Very funny." I smirked and entered the shop to

the sound of yapping pups.

Sheba went to investigate while I checked emails to see whether we had any boarders for the next day. Not seeing anything pressing, I searched the internet for any mention of a cat burglar in Waterfall. I'd sink myself into crime to forget about the snake.

A small article in the local breaking news. A painting had disappeared from the country club in the neighboring city of Silver Brook. I guessed that if the same person who stole the woman's ruby ring at the wedding had taken the painting, we might have a cat burglar on our hands, but it seemed like a stretch to me.

We knew who had Heather's earrings. Mr. Jennings. The question was why were they in his possession? Had he taken them, or had the person who killed him planted the earrings on him?

I turned off my computer. Far too many questions.

My cell phone rang. I snatched it off the counter. "Hey, Shar."

"I'm missing the bracelet Alex gave me for Christmas. The back door was unlocked and hung open when I returned home."

I snatched my keys off the counter, slung my purse over my shoulder, and called to Sheba as I raced out the door. Once in my car, I sent Brad a quick text about where I was going, then sped toward Shar's house.

Who would steal from the house where a detective spent most of his time? Sure, Alex didn't live there officially, but he spent most of his nights with my friend. Maybe Shar misplaced the bracelet. Not likely, since she treasured the gift, but it was possible.

I found her on the sofa in tears. "Did you call Alex?"

"He didn't answer his phone."

"Are you sure it's missing?"

"Of course, I am." She glared, wiping her eyes. "I keep it in my jewelry box and look at it several times a day. The entire box is gone."

That changed things. "You shouldn't have come inside knowing someone broke in. It's dangerous."

"Pshaw. I have my gun in my purse. This is personal, Trinity. We need to find whoever this cat burglar is and get my bracelet back."

We didn't have a clue where to start except for questioning those who worked with David. Maybe one of them would know who wanted Jennings dead. Too late in the day to do anything, and with Heather on her honeymoon, taking off work in the middle of the day was impossible.

"What are you thinking?" Shar asked.

I told her what went through my mind. "We can't do anything until Heather comes back the day after tomorrow."

"She comes home tonight."

"But doesn't start work until day after tomorrow. I'm not calling her in early."

"Fine." She jumped up and started pacing. "Let's find out where Jennings' kids live. We can question them."

"Their father was just murdered." I hated always being the voice of reason.

"Are you going to help or not?" She whipped around to face me.

"Yes, I am, but we can't do anything right now." But soon, we would find out who took her bracelet and killed Mr. Jennings.

Chapter Four

Heather wasn't very excited that Shar and I wanted to take off early on her first day back. "I wanted to tell you about my honeymoon."

"You told us last night at your gift opening," Shar said, slinging her oversized bag over her arm.

"There's a lot more to tell." She frowned.

"We'll catch up, I promise." I gave her a hug.

"Why don't you sell this place and apply for your investigator license?" She slammed a dog dish on the shelf she stocked. "I'm here more than you are."

"I'm sorry."

She waved a hand in my direction. "Don't mind me. I'm being silly. The police need your help. You're good at this." She stepped back. "I can handle things here this afternoon. I'm just surly because my wonderful honeymoon is over, and it's back to normal life. Robbie's grandparents spoiled him so badly he's become a little tyrant."

I laughed. "Welcome home."

She smiled. "Go find Shar's bracelet."

Since I'd done some digging on the internet, I knew the names of Mr. Jennings' children and found their addresses. Scary how much information a person can find online.

Shar insisted on driving, and since she refused to let any dog but her poodle, Starr, in her vintage Thunderbird, I left Sheba behind. "Sorry, but she's so big," she said.

"That's why I prefer driving." I scooted Starr over so I could climb into the front passenger seat. "All she does is spread across the backseat. It's not like she chews the upholstery."

"Sheba scares people. We're visiting grieving folks today who don't need to be startled by a monster dog." She turned the key in the ignition, then pulled away from the store.

"She only looks dangerous." I crossed my arms and glared at the storefront window where my big fur baby looked out. "From now on, I drive everywhere."

"Fine." She cut me a glance. "There must be something in the air. First Heather, now you."

I shrugged. Why did it bother me so much to leave Sheba behind once in a while? "I'm sorry. I'm acting like a petulant teenager."

"What's bothering you?"

I hesitated but decided I needed to talk with someone. "You can't say a word."

"Okay. You know if you tell me it's a secret, I won't say anything. But if you don't—"

"It's a secret." I narrowed my eyes. "At the wedding, I was just about to tell Brad I'd set a date for the wedding when I spotted that darn cat, then found the dead guy."

"Yay!" She grinned and drove down the exit to the interstate. "It's about time."

"Look who's talking. What about you and Alex?"

"I'm going to kidnap him and elope."

I widened my eyes, then burst out laughing. "You can't kidnap a detective and force him to marry you."

"Watch me." She arched a brow. "So, why didn't you tell Brad later?"

"Every time I started to, something happened. Maybe we aren't meant to get married."

"Don't be an idiot. The universe isn't trying to keep you apart."

"No, but God might be. What if I'm not wife material? All this gallivanting around we do can't be good for a marriage."

"Brad comes along at least half the time. Stop making excuses and marry that gorgeous man."

I nodded. "I will. Turn right at the next exit, then right again. The closest son is Shane Jennings. If he doesn't want to talk to us, we respect that and leave. Understand?"

"Yes, ma'am."

"I'm serious."

"Right. Don't try to press on if they say no." She nodded.

Shane Jennings lived in a forty-year-old ranch home on a hill. He stood from where he'd sat in a rocking chair on the porch when we pulled up. Suspenders held up jeans straining under a round belly. He swiped at a stain on his white tee-shirt, then set aside a jar of what looked like tea.

I shoved open my door and stepped onto a gravel driveway. "Mr. Jennings?"

"Yep. Who are you?"

"Trinity Ashford. I, uh, discovered your father's body."

"Okay." He frowned. "What do you need?"

"This is my friend Sharon Carpenter. We're helping the authorities find out who killed your father. Do you have a few minutes to answer some questions? We'd like to visit your brother later."

"No need. He's here. We're planning the funeral. Dane?"

A thinner, but otherwise identical version of Shane, stepped out of the house. He shot us a suspicious look but joined his brother on the edge of the porch.

"These ladies want to talk to us about Dad," Shane said.

Dane shrugged. "Come on up, then." He headed to a rocking chair and sat, pushing the chair into motion with his big toe.

His brother took the other chair, leaving a weathered porch swing for Shar and me to share. I moved a moldy throw pillow and took my seat.

I swallowed against a suddenly dry throat. "I'm…we're sorry for your loss. If this is a bad time—"

"There ain't no good time," Shane said. "Ask your questions." He reached for the jar, not offering us any.

"Do you know of anyone who disliked your father enough to kill him?" Might as well be direct and move on.

"Probably most of his employees. Our father wasn't the nicest fella on the block."

"Yeah," Dane added. "He could be gruff. Wanted everything done just so."

David had never said anything bad about his boss. We'd have to question him a little more. "A lot of bosses are rough. Doesn't mean anyone wants to kill them."

"That's right." Shar leaned forward. "We're upsetting people all the time, yet here we are."

I really didn't know what to say to that. We'd had multiple people try to kill us. I opened my mouth and closed it a few times.

"Looks like the younger girl is speechless," Dane said. "Never seen such a sight. Most women don't know how to stay quiet."

"She's usually talking a mile a minute." Shar smiled. "But, we don't want to take up too much of your time, gentlemen. Your father also had some stolen earrings in his possession."

"Stolen?" Shane shot to his feet. "You accusing him of being a thief?"

Leave it to Shar. I put a hand on her arm. "Missing earrings, not stolen. I'm sure he found them and intended to give them to the DJ, so an announcement could be made." I wasn't sure of any such thing but didn't need a fight to erupt.

The man barely looked pacified but reclaimed his seat. "My old man had enough money. He wouldn't stoop to stealing. He just preferred to do things different."

"Like underhanded business dealings," Dane

said. "All perfectly legal but maybe not ethical. He bought that delivery service right out from under the nose of a little old lady when her husband died suddenly. Bought it for nothing close to what it was worth. That's the kind of man he was."

"Looks like the two of you will benefit," Shar said.

Shane scowled her way. "You aren't real good with nice talk, are you?"

"No, she isn't." I shot Shar a warning look, then turned my attention back to Shane. "So it appears the police should focus their attention on people your father did business with."

"That's what I would do. Told them that, when they came by to question us after his death. Didn't seem to do much good. They haven't caught anyone." He glanced at his watch. "We have an appointment at the funeral home."

Our cue to leave. I stood and offered my hand. "Again, sorry for your loss."

He wrapped a meaty, calloused hand around mine. "Thank you." Then, he released my hand and ambled into the house, his brother following.

Back in the car, I turned to Shar. "Has David ever said anything bad about Mr. Jennings?"

"Not that I know of. He doesn't talk about work much, and when he comes in with a delivery, he focuses on Heather."

"Hm. Let's stop by Jennings Delivery." We had time since the two brothers had been in the same place.

We arrived just as David headed for his car after work. Shar beeped the horn, attracting his attention.

Smiling, he changed direction. "Hello, ladies. What's up?"

"We heard that Mr. Jennings wasn't nice to his employees," Shar blurted out.

"You really need a muzzle, you know that?" I frowned. "But, yes, that's what we heard, David."

He leaned on the car, then straightened at Shar's glare. "He was tough, but as long as you did your job, he didn't come down on you. I wouldn't call that mean."

Neither would I. "No altercations between him and one of the employees?"

He shrugged. "Not that I know of, but as a delivery driver, I was rarely in the office. Wait a sec. I did hear an argument a few days before the wedding. Between him and a vendor, I think. A man's voice. I had a delivery to make so didn't stick around. It wasn't any of my business."

"Can you get a list of those vendors?" I asked.

"I guess, but wouldn't I be doing something illegal?"

"I don't know." I grinned. "Come on, live dangerously."

"I'll get it from the secretary tomorrow and drop it by the store. I'd better not end up behind bars." He glowered and strode to his truck.

Shar rubbed her hands together. "Now we're talking. We'll have a whole list of suspects to question."

One of which might be the person who killed Jennings. Asking questions could put us six-feet under, too.

CYNTHIA HICKEY

Chapter Five

The receptionist at David's office took off half a day, so he didn't receive the list until closing time at Tail Waggin'. He set several sheets of paper on the counter. "I'd better not lose my job over this."

"You're starting to sound like a broken record," Shar said. "Besides, I already told Alex our plans."

"What did he say?" I glanced her way.

"To stay out of it, but I could tell from his voice that he knew we wouldn't. That's the same as giving me the okay." She grabbed her purse and headed for the door. "Now, I guess we'll have to wait until morning to do anything."

Which was fine with me. I had plans to walk around the lake with Brad that evening with no company other than our dogs. "See you tomorrow." I folded the vendor list and slipped it into my purse. "Thanks, David."

He nodded, his attention fully on Heather now. "Ready?"

"Yes." Her eyes shone.

I sighed and watched them waltz out of the store, clearly having forgotten about me. Seeing how deeply in love they were had me itching to tell Brad that evening at the lake that I'd set a date. No more waiting. It would be a rush to set everything up in a little under two months, but I could do it. I'd always wanted to be a June bride.

Speaking of marriage, my hunky future groom headed my way, a wicker basket hanging on one arm, the other occupied with a twirling beagle. He stopped to put the basket and Barney in his car.

"Come on, Sheba. Let's have a picnic." I locked up the store and joined Brad, lifting my face for a kiss.

"Missed you." He obliged with a peck on my nose.

"Same." I smiled and let Sheba into the backseat with Barney. Poor girl still barely tolerated the playful dog and curled up, casting me a forlorn look. I laughed and closed the door.

We made small talk about our day until we reached the lake. "Let's walk to the far side," Brad suggested. "Fewer people."

"Sounds perfect." I took the dogs' leashes, leaving him the basket and an old quilt. "I love May. The temperature couldn't be more perfect."

"I agree." He smiled my way. "You have a secret."

"Why do you say that?"

"Because it's written all over your face."

I grinned. "I'll tell you later." I almost blurted it out on the walking trail but wanted it to be memorable. So, to divert his attention, I mentioned the vendor list.

"Let me see it when we find our spot. I might know some of them. If I do, they might be more willing to talk if I'm with you."

"Good idea."

We found a thick patch of grass under an oak tree. Brad spread out the quilt and I unhooked the dogs' leashes. Both were trained enough they wouldn't venture far. Especially once the food came out.

I removed the vendor list from my purse and handed it to Brad. He scanned the pages of businesses.

"I know a few of these. I'll be glad to help. Most of Waterfall used Jennings Delivery."

"All we're doing is asking how they felt about Jennings. See if they act suspicious." I opened the basket and removed cheeses, crackers, fruit, and sausage. "Wine?"

He smiled and took a glass. "You can find out how they felt on your own. Why not wait until the funeral and scope people out then?"

"Why not do both? If one of the vendors seems shady, I'll know who to watch closely at the funeral." I rarely drink wine except for special occasions. What did Brad have up his sleeve? "You can take the ones you know, and Shar and I will take the others. Circle yours." I dug a pen from my purse. "I'll make a copy in the morning and give it to you when you bring the coffee. Is that all right?"

"Sounds good to me." He circled several names, then stretched out, resting on his elbow. "Trinity, I'm tired of wait—"

"June fifth."

"What?" He sat up, confusion shadowing his eyes.

"What were you going to say?"

"That I'm tired of waiting to buy a house. I found a gorgeous, fixer-upper Victorian on fifteen acres of land. You'll have your little farm."

"That's what the wine is for?"

He nodded. "What is June fifth?"

I started laughing. Tears ran down my face. "Our...wedding...day." I fell over, clutching my stomach and stared through the tree branches at the darkening sky. "I wanted it...to be romantic, not hysterical."

Joining me in laughter, he lay beside me, our arms touching. "You bring me so much joy, Trinity Ashford."

"Does the date sound okay?"

"I'd marry you tonight if you'd let me. The date doesn't matter." He took my hand and pulled me over for a kiss.

I had a lot of work to do to put a wedding together in six weeks. Something fell on my back. I tugged myself away from Brad's kisses and stared into Sheba's big face. "You have bad timing, girl."

She made a snuffling sound and sat, her gaze glued on me. Dirt covered her paws and nose.

"She brought you something." Brad held up a floral sack stained with dirt. He untied the drawstring and looked inside. "Found Shar's bracelet and quite a few other things."

I yanked the bag out of his hand and stared inside at a fortune. "Who is dumb enough to hide this many stolen jewels in the ground by a private lake?"

"I doubt they expected a dog to dig them up. Hurry and put it inside the picnic basket. I hear someone coming."

Shoving it in the basket, I closed the lid as two men appeared around the bend. I picked up a piece of cheese and took a bite, then held a grape to Brad's lips, keeping with the lovers' picnic theme.

They barely glanced our way, instead, heading toward the lake. When they reached the water's edge, they turned right into the trees. It didn't take long for them to rush back into sight.

By now, Brad had poured the wine, and we watched the show over the rim of our glasses. "They do not look happy," he whispered.

"Nope."

They glanced around the area, then came our way, stopping a few feet away when Sheba planted herself between them and us. "Is she friendly?" The taller one asked.

"Unless commanded," I said. "Can we help you?"

"Anyone out here other than you two?"

Brad shrugged. "Not that we've noticed, but we're kind of involved in each other right now. Just set our wedding date. Now, we're celebrating." He raised his glass. "No reason to pay attention to anyone else."

Tall Man peered back to the stand of trees he and his buddy had come from. "Can't see anything from here," he told the other guy.

"Must have gone in and come out some other

way," the shorter man said. "Sorry to have bothered y'all." He turned and dashed back the way from which he'd come, the taller one on his heels.

"Do we call McIlroy or pack up and take it with us?"

"I say we call." He dug his phone from his pocket. "They'll want to see where the dogs dug up the bag and take prints from where the men walked."

True. I wanted to go take a look myself but didn't feel up to a lecture from the detective about trampling a potential crime scene. So, I returned to eating and watching the golden sunset on the lake kiss the surface of the water. A slight breeze blew, bringing the scent of lake water and Brad's cologne to my nostrils.

"He'll be here with Officer Snowe in about fifteen minutes."

"Great. What a way to ruin a wonderful evening."

Brad chuckled. "We didn't do anything wrong—didn't stick our noses where they don't belong, so there's no reason for them to be upset with us."

We'd finished eating and I'd returned the leftovers to the basket by the time McIlroy and Snowe marched up the path. Brad handed them the bag of jewels. "All we did was look inside. The dogs dug it up somewhere in those trees."

"I'll see if I can find out where," Snowe said, heading that way.

Brad then told the detective about the two men who'd clearly been looking for something. "They seemed to believe we didn't have anything to do with whatever they were looking for."

"Let's hope so. If they are the thieves, you'd be in danger."

"Wouldn't be the first time." I gave a wry grin. "We weren't doing anything but celebrating the fact Brad bought a house and we set a date. See how these things just happen?"

"Only to you. No one else in Waterfall is neck deep in trouble every couple of months." He shook his head and turned as Snowe came back.

"I found the hole. Two sets of prints, not counting the dogs'. Want me to contain the scene?"

"Yes." McIlroy turned his attention back to us. "I suggest the two of you leave. The media will be here, and if you're seen on the news, those men will know you found the stolen items."

Brad stood and folded the quilt while I put the dogs back on their leashes. We returned to our cars.

I froze next to the vehicle, catching sight of the two men standing next to a beat-up red Chevy pickup. "Why do you think the police are here?" I said, loudly.

Brad's brow furrowed, then smoothed as I made a slight jerk of my head toward the two men. "I don't know, but we packed up just in time, it seems." He opened the trunk and stored the blanket and basket. "Want to stick around and see?"

"Do you guys know what's going on?" I called out, letting the dogs into the car.

They each shook their head, their gaze flicking from us to the path.

"Okay, we might as well go then. Have a good

evening." I jumped into the car and locked the door.

Brad's eyes darted to the rearview mirror as he drove away. "They're following."

"Are you sure? There isn't anywhere to turn off right now."

"We'll find out soon enough. If they are, I'm taking you home with me. The penthouse is safer than your apartment."

No argument here. I peered over my seat as we left the road leading to the lake. The truck had several opportunities to turn off the road. When we arrived in town, there was no question they were following us.

"I don't think they believed us for a second that we didn't have their jewels."

Nodding, Brad's gaze flicked back to the mirror. "They saw right through us."

"I bet they noticed the dirt on Sheba." They couldn't have missed it with the way she planted herself in front of them.

"Regardless, they can't follow us into the parking garage unless they park and walk in." He pressed the remote hanging from the car's visor and pulled into the garage, lowering the bar behind him. "Let's hurry."

I grabbed the dogs while he collected the things from the trunk, then we raced for the elevator. Brad pressed the button for the penthouse. The doors opened, and we hurried inside his place, locking the door behind us.

The tension fell from my shoulders. We were safe. At least for the moment.

Chapter Six

Heather waved us away before I had a change to complete my sentence about Shar and me meeting up with my mother to visit vendors. "I got it."

"If you'd let me finish…" I glared, "you'd hear me say I'm doing most of the investigating in the store on the phone. If I need to, I'll take off early."

"Sorry." She gave a sheepish grin. "I shouldn't assume."

It was justified since I did take off a lot during a mystery. "I'll be in the back office unless you need me." I took my purse, the coffee Brad dropped off earlier, and the list with me to the office I rarely used. Small, windowless, it barely had room for the small glass-topped desk, filing cabinet, rolling chair, and one other foldable chair I usually kept propped against the wall. Maybe some decorations would make the claustrophobic space feel homier.

"I want to help." Shar pouted in the doorway.

"You said you have several grooming appointments today."

"I do, but I'll be gone most of the day since these are mobile ones."

"I'll try not to have too much fun without you." I took a sip of my drink. "Close the door, please. I promise to fill you in on anything I find out."

First call was to Mullens Paper Products. I introduced myself when the receptionist answered the phone, then asked to speak with anyone who had the time to answer questions about Jennings.

"Are you a private investigator?" she asked. "Because other than law enforcement, I cannot speak about our clients."

"The manager perhaps?"

"You didn't say you wanted to ask me a question about the manager."

I shoved down a groan. "May I speak with the manager?"

"One moment, please."

Elevator music replaced her voice. I leaned back and drummed my fingers on the desktop.

"This is Mullens."

"Mr. Mullens, I'm Trinity Ashford from Tail Waggin' Daycare and Spa. I'm hoping to ask you a few questions about Mr. Jennings."

"You should have asked for a reference before he died, Miss. Too late now."

Okay. In person would have definitely been better than on the phone. "Yes, of course, but I'm calling to ask about the man not his business. I'm investigating his death."

Silence vibrated the airwaves. Then, a clearing of the man's throat. "I don't like to speak ill of the dead, but Jennings wasn't a good businessman.

Died with several unpaid bills. You might want to start there as to who might want to kill him."

"Where would I find that information?"

"His sons, I reckon."

"Did he have unpaid bills with you?"

"Yes, but I didn't kill him. Kind of hard for a man in a wheelchair to shove a body under a buffet table. My guess is you're looking for someone large. Good day, Miss Ashford. Good luck in your endeavor." Click.

Next call...Shane Jennings. "I'm staring at a pile of unpaid bills right now trying to figure out what to do with them all. I really don't want to sell the business, but I might not have another choice."

"Can you tell me who he owed money to, giving me the name of who he owed the most?"

"That would be Mills over at the hardware store. Dad was doing some renovations, still incomplete. He owes Mills close to two thousand dollars. The others are utility bills, gas bills, bills for supplies." He rattled off names and dollar amounts. "Dane and I were talking last night about the earrings found on Dad. What if he had resorted to stealing in order to get money to pay off his debt?"

"That's a thought. Thank you, Shane. You've been terrific." I hung up and stared at the empty wall opposite me. Shane could be right. What if his father had entered into a partnership with the town's elusive cat burglar and something went wrong?

I dialed McIlroy's number.

"What did you do now?" he asked.

"Nothing." I told him my theory.

"We've considered that. Don't irritate the

vendors. If one of them killed Mr. Jennings, they'd never reclaim their money."

Good point. Which put me back at square one without a suspect. "Maybe one of the vendors is the cat burglar."

"Good luck finding that out." He hung up.

Sometimes, Shar's boyfriend could be very rude. Now I had a new angle to pursue with no idea what the first step should be. I sent Brad a text informing him that calling the vendors was most likely a bad idea.

He replied almost immediately that I was wrong because he'd seen one of the men from the lake enter the building belonging to Waterfall Waterworks. I glanced at my list. Jennings had owed three-hundred dollars for plumbing work.

I called Brad. "Does the business look as if it's hurting for business?"

"It's in a rundown part of town, so maybe. They could just like the cheaper rent. I hadn't gotten out of the car yet when I spotted the guy. Now I'm waiting for him to come back out."

"How long has it been?"

"Half an hour."

If he worked there, Brad could be waiting all day. "Keep me posted."

"I'm thinking about getting some plumbing done at the theater. See if I can't flush out a rat."

"That'll do it, especially since those two men saw us." We disconnected the call. Again, I drummed my fingers on the desk. Finding a cat burglar and a killer, which may or may not be the same person, was not going to be easy.

Sure, we'd seen two men searching for something at the lake. But it didn't mean they stole or killed. Maybe someone did it for them. Maybe Waterfall had a whole ring of thieves. We had our work cut out for us.

I sighed and pushed to my feet. McIlroy didn't seem to think the vendors were relevant, but Mr. Mills was two doors down. It wouldn't hurt for me to pay the hardware store a visit.

I stopped in the front room at the sight of Heather quietly crying. "What happened?"

"David was let go from work. The company is folding."

I wrapped my arms around her. "David will find another job. I'll ask Brad to help. He knows most of the business owners around."

"That's true." She sniffed and wiped her eyes on her sleeve. "I'm being silly. It isn't the end of the world, only unexpected."

"Will you be all right if I head to the hardware store for a few minutes?"

"I'll be fine."

I texted Brad about David on my way to the hardware store. He replied that he'd already found David employment because, while not common knowledge yet, he'd offered to buy Jennings Delivery and make David the manager.

Oh, how I loved my rich man. I texted back that he was a saint, then continued on my quest with a spring in my step. A bell jingled over the door as I entered. Mr. Mills was waiting on a customer and called out that he would be right with me.

Since I wasn't the type of gal to be interested in

nuts and bolts, I idly wandered the aisles. When I'd made the rounds and the customer still stood at the counter, I crossed my arms and leaned against the opposite end of the counter. Spotting a display I hadn't seen in his store before, I pushed away and went to the front of the store.

A red desk lamp stood on top of its empty box. A desk pad with a flowered border sat propped against another box. "When did you start carrying office supplies?" I asked over my shoulder.

"Last week. Cut a good deal. Be with you in a minute."

I grabbed the lamp and desk pad. My first purchases to a more pleasing office. I set them on the counter and listened as Mr. Mills told the customer how to fit together PVC pipes and little black thingies that would drip water onto plants. Sprinkler system, maybe?

Finally, the man left, and Mr. Mills turned to me. "That it?" He motioned to the items in front of me.

"To purchase, yes. I'd like to ask you a few questions about Mr. Jennings." I smiled even knowing that kindness rarely worked to my benefit with the surly Mr. Mills.

"Nosing around again?" His brows lowered.

"Yep. I heard he owes you a lot of money."

"You heard right."

"I also know you'll be receiving that money." If Brad bought out Jennings, he'd make sure all debts were paid. "What did you think about the man?"

"Go back to me getting my money."

"I can't tell you anything more."

"Maybe I can't tell you anything then." He crossed his arms.

I copied. "Just trust me."

"Jennings was a flake. Spouted off promises, then never followed through. Heard he had a gambling problem which is why he's broke, but that's hearsay." He rang up my purchases.

"Heard anything about a cat burglar?"

"A cat that steals things or a person who's really good at breaking in and out undetected?"

"The second."

"Only what I've read in the paper. You owe me seventeen fifty."

I handed him a twenty. "Any idea who might have wanted him dead?"

He laughed without humor. "People he owed money to. If he did have a gambling problem, maybe he borrowed money from someone he shouldn't have, couldn't pay, and they killed him."

Another avenue to pursue. That one I'd gladly let McIlroy handle. I had no desire to get involved with loan sharks. "Thanks."

"Be careful. You won't always skate by, just out of reach."

His words made my skin prickle. I'd often wondered the same. How many times would death come knocking and I walked away?

I decided to make one more trip and entered the thrift store. Mrs. Murdoch would have a picture or two to hang on my office wall.

"Good morning." She popped up from behind the counter. "What are you looking for today?"

"Pictures to hang on my office wall. I'm

decorating."

"What about movie posters? I have one of Marilyn Monroe and one of *Gone With the Wind*. Framed and ready to go."

I followed her to the back of the store. The posters were perfect. "I love them."

"There's a tape dispenser in the shape of a stiletto on that shelf. That would look cute on your desk. Or maybe you prefer animals? Of course, you do. Here's one that's a cat." She added it to my purchases. "Anything else?"

"That'll do." I chuckled and followed her back to the counter.

"Heard you found Mr. Jennings' body." She rang up my purchases. "Sad thing for the maid of honor to find."

"Weren't you there?"

"No, I meant to go, but my stomach was ailing me. I didn't mind missing that kind of excitement."

"Did you know Mr. Jennings?"

"Most everyone who's been here any length of time does. He wasn't...nice. Not horrible, but tolerable. Jennings changed after the death of his wife ten years ago. Car accident. He was driving. He'd been drinking and ran a stop sign. T-boned by a big truck. Anyway, he started drinking more, his business suffered, and his boys didn't have much to do with him."

"I heard he might have had a gambling problem." I gripped the handle of the bag holding the tape dispenser and hefted the posters under one arm.

"Possibly. Heard that, too, but since I don't visit

the casino in Oklahoma, I wouldn't know for a fact."

"Thanks." I carried my things back to the store and into the office, before heading back to let Heather know everything would be fine. I didn't tell her the reason, only that Brad had everything under control.

"That's a relief. We wouldn't make it long on just my income." She continued stocking dog food.

"Find out anything worthwhile?" Shar asked, coming from the grooming room.

"Looks like a trip to the casino is on the list."

She clapped. "I love the casino."

"Jennings might have shared the same love. We'll go after the funeral tomorrow." I'd already made up a sign saying the store would be closed when Brad barged into the store.

"Both of the men from the lake work at Waterfall Plumbing," he said. "They're both plumbers. How much do you want to bet they go into homes to fix something and scout out the place?" He glanced at Shar. "Have any plumbing done recently?"

Her eyes widened. "Sure did. Two days before my bracelet went missing."

All we had to do know was prove our theory correct.

Chapter Seven

I knelt and gave Sheba a hug. "Not this time, sweetie. A funeral is no place for a dog. I promise to come let you outside for a bit before heading to the casino." I so often took her with me investigating that I felt guilty when I couldn't. "Plus, a big snack."

I stepped out my door and turned to lock it. A snake coiled at my feet. I jumped back and screamed before looking closer. A rubber snake?

Brad laughed at the bottom of the stairs.

"Not funny. I have anxiety over that snake in the boat, and you want to play tricks?" I tossed the snake in the bushes and stomped down the stairs.

Still snickering, he followed me and opened the passenger side door so I could slide in. "It is kind of funny. You'll never get over your fright if you don't laugh about it."

"Oh, now you're a psychiatrist?" I arched a brow and swept the hem of my navy-blue dress under me.

"You're cute when you're mad." He closed the

door and loped to the driver's side.

Cute, my foot. I wanted to strangle him.

He leaned over and kissed me. My anger melted away.

"Not fair." I pretended to pout. "You know I can't stay mad when you kiss me."

"That's the idea." Grinning, he started the car.

The smile didn't leave my face until we pulled into the lot of the funeral home. With what I'd heard about Jennings, I hadn't expected the lot to be full, but Brad had to drive to the back of the building to find a spot to park.

Shar waited next to her Thunderbird and waved. "Alex is already inside. He's on duty. You know the killer will show up. They always do."

"Not everything is like the movies." I fell into step beside her, Brad right behind as we entered through the back door.

"Is it all right if I speak with Shane and Dane?" Brad asked. "They asked me to find them when I arrived."

Thinking it strange they'd want to talk business at their father's funeral, I nodded. "Shar and I will mingle."

"Look for anyone shifty." Shar narrowed her eyes.

"They won't be that obvious." I shook my head. "There's the two men Brad and I saw at the lake. Was one of them the plumber that fixed your pipes?"

"I wasn't there. I told the gal on the phone where the key would be. The plumber came while I was at work."

I widened my eyes. "You should've asked for the time off."

"Don't look at me like that. Everyone does it—leaves their key. It's only recently that our town has had such a crime spree. Oh, snacks." She made a beeline for a sideboard loaded with cakes, cookies, finger sandwiches, and a pitcher of sweet tea and one of lemonade.

I poured a glass of lemonade and moseyed through the crowd of people to get closer to the men from the lake. It might be cliché, but a silk tree provided some protection from being spotted.

"They're going to start putting the pieces together," one of the men said. "We have to stop stealing from houses we're working on. The thefts need to be random."

"How do you propose we do that, Bill? The people letting us in is how we gain access."

"I don't know, Ted. Maybe you'll have to think about that. Use the brain rattling around in your skull."

I smiled around the rim of my glass. Trouble in paradise, fellas? Uh oh. I pretended to pick something up off the floor as the men passed my hiding place.

"What are you doing?" McIlroy stared through the branches of the silk tree. "Spying?"

"Trying to." I straightened. "You shouldn't sneak up on someone like that."

"You're very obvious."

"I am not. This is a lovely painting on the wall. I've been admiring it."

"Stop nosing around. I mean it." He let the

branches fall back into place.

With a sigh, I left the corner I'd taken refuge in and went in search of Shar, Brad, or the two men—whomever I might come across first.

"Pssst." Shar waved from the women's restroom.

I joined her, and she slammed the door, planting her body against it. "You'll never guess what I found out."

"The identity of the killer?" I arched a brow, then refreshed my peach lipstick in the gold-framed mirror hanging over a marble sink and vanity. Why did funeral homes have such luxurious bathrooms?

"The names of the men from the lake."

"Bill and Ted?"

"Oh, pooh. You're a real pill, Trinity."

I smiled. "They're going to think of new ways of getting into houses."

"You heard them say they're doing the stealing? Did you record them?"

"Unfortunately, I did not." Which meant it was my word against theirs. "They're not cat burglars. Just plain old thieves. What we have to do is prove it."

"Did they say anything about Jennings?"

"No." I dotted my lips with a tissue. "Maybe they didn't kill him."

"A third bad guy?" Her mouth fell open. "A boss thief?"

"We don't have all the answers yet. Let's not speculate." Although, it made sense there might be a third party involved. "Has McIlroy said how the department is doing on the wedding guest list and the servers?"

"He won't tell me anything."

"Then it's up to us to find the answers." I left the restroom and sat beside Brad as the pastor took his place behind the podium. "Find out anything?"

"I'll take possession of the business on Monday. The brothers are selling everything here and moving to Texas." He cut me a sideways glance. "When do you want to see the house I bought?"

"As soon as possible." I slipped my hand into his. "Since Shar and I are going to the casino, how about tomorrow?"

"Sounds perfect." He gave my hand a squeeze and turned his attention to the pastor.

After a short lesson on heaven, the pastor released us. The burial would be only for immediate family.

"So much for finding the killer," Shar leaned over and whispered. "I say we go to the cemetery anyway. Pretend to be visiting a different grave. If someone other than the brothers show up, well, bam. That's our killer."

"You really are a bit loopy, aren't you?" Brad smiled to take some of the sting out of his words.

"It works in the movies." She plopped back into her seat, elbowing McIlroy in the stomach. "Sorry."

"I'm in love with a crazy person." He rubbed his belly. "Try not to get into trouble at the casino, okay? I have enough to do."

As we left, I spotted Heather and David sitting in the back row. "Y'all came in late?"

She nodded. "Robbie wasn't cooperating. Nice service, even if a short one."

"I bought Jennings Delivery, David. I'd like to hire you as the manager, if you're interested."

"Really?" David jumped to his feet. "Are you serious?"

Brad chuckled. "Very serious. I know you can do the job. See me at eight o'clock Monday morning at the office. We'll talk particulars."

"It was nice of you to buy the delivery business and save those people's jobs." I linked my arm with Brad's.

"It's also good business sense." He winked at me.

Right. He had a heart as big as the Ozark Mountains, but hadn't earned his riches by giving things away. Brad did donate to various charities, but I couldn't help but admire his business sense. "Do you want to grab a quick lunch at my place before you head to work?"

"Sure. Let's pick up some burgers."

When we arrived back at my place, Brad took Sheba out to do her business while I changed into jeans and a tee-shirt. If I was going to be losing money, I wanted to be comfortable doing it. Yes, we were going to ask questions about Jennings, but I loved the lights, the noise, the fake jingle of coins falling when someone hit a jackpot. I took only the amount of money I wouldn't cringe at losing.

Dressed, I set out the burgers and fries. Shar would pick me up in a bit, but I had some time.

"Do you know when you'll be back?" Brad asked.

"I'm not sure. Before dark, I hope. I'll call you." I bit into my bacon cheeseburger.

"I should take you to Vegas sometime if you like casinos. Ever been?"

I shook my head. "That might be dangerous."

"There is more to do than just hit the slots." He laughed. "Just let me know if you want to go."

"Oh, I would love to."

When Shar honked out front, Brad leaned over and kissed me. "Have fun. Don't worry about the animals. I'll take care of them. Be careful. You might ask the right question to the wrong person."

"It isn't too late for you to come along."

"You girls have fun. I'll be waiting when you come back." Another kiss, and he followed me from the apartment, locking the door behind us.

"Let's hit the road!" Shar had the convertible's top down and a scarf tied around her hair.

"You trying to be Audrey Hepburn?" I slid into the passenger seat.

"It keeps my hair from becoming a tangled mess. There's another one in the glove compartment. Of course, I doubt anyone could tell the difference with your hair. It always looks messy."

"My hair is wavy, not messy." I took out the pink and green scarf and tied it around my hair. With my oversized sunglasses, the two of us resembled movie stars from the Golden age. Maybe I shouldn't have worn jeans. Shar wore an elegant pair of linen slacks with a matching tunic.

"We're making a pit stop." Shar turned into the police department parking lot and honked.

Mom came running out, purse slung over her shoulder. "You didn't forget about me, unlike some people." She shot me a dirty look.

"I thought you had to work." I shrugged.

"I can take time off once in a while."

"You're right. I'm a horrible daughter." I settled back against the seat as Mom slid in the back seat. "Want up front?"

"No, thank you. I'm fine back here."

"Have you and Dad taken the boat out again?"

"This past weekend. We want to go out every weekend while the weather permits. I'm happy to say we saw no snakes."

I shuddered. "I'm not going back anytime soon."

"You'll face down murderers but not a little ole snake."

"That's right." It sounded strange spoken out loud, but I couldn't help my phobia of snakes, spiders, bugs—things a girl in Arkansas came across on a regular basis. "Let's make a plan. Are we going to split up or stay together?"

"If we make it look like three gals out for an afternoon of fun, we won't look suspicious," Mom said. "The casino workers might be more willing to talk to us."

"I agree," Shar said. "Keep it light and easy. Hey, I'll teach the two of you to play roulette. Makes your money last longer than the one-armed bandit."

"Alex said if we run across the killer, we are"—and he raised his voice when he said this—"we are not to confront the person." Mom tied a scarf around her hair. "Said to leave the casino and call him. I told him we could do that, but not before one of us snapped the person's picture. Oh, the ranting that man can do."

"Welcome to my world." Shar laughed.

I agreed with McIlroy this time. No engaging with a suspected killer.

Chapter Eight

Shar parked the Thunderbird away from other cars to avoid anyone slamming a door into the side, which left us with a football field of distance to walk. I followed the two glamour gals feeling very much like a luggage attendant tagging along behind celebrities.

At the casino entrance, they whipped off their scarves and shook out their hair, pausing for effect. Me, I could barely contain my excitement at the lights and sounds.

Mom shot out an arm to stop me from rushing ahead. "Slow your roll, dear. Take it all in. Formulate a plan. See whether anyone is paying us more attention than they should."

"That's what the celebrity act is all about?" I scanned the room. Other than the security guards, no one spared us a glance. "Let's play for a bit before interrogating people, okay?"

"I wish you'd made an attempt with your appearance." Mom eyed my jeans. "You can't flirt with the guard dressed like that."

WEDDING DAY CAT BURGLAR

"Who said anything about flirting?"

"Who in this place would know Jennings if he was a regular?" She tilted her head. "The guards."

"So you go ask questions."

"You're younger."

"Fine. Then can I go play? I know we're here to find a clue as to who killed Jennings, but blending in would be the best start. Right now, those guards are staring at us with suspicion in their eyes."

"I suppose we'll have to hit the slots for a while, then you can come back and ask some questions." Shar, head high, strolled through the machines until she found one that called to her.

Since there was an empty seat across from her, I sat down and inserted my member card, then the slip of paper with my credits. I rubbed my hands together and pulled the handle. Round and round and round...nothing. To change things up, I pressed the spin button. "Yes!" I won five dollars.

"That would've been a lot more if you were playing the maximum bid." An older woman sat next to me. "You must be new here."

"Maybe once a year." I changed my bid to max and pressed the button again. I won my bid back. "Do you come here often?"

"More than I should." She smiled. "My husband passed away last year. We used to come here a lot together. He left me a tidy sum of money, so I spend one day a week here."

"Did you know a Mr. Jennings?"

"Sure did. Heard someone killed him."

I'd hit the jackpot without resorting to flirting. "Knife to the chest. Did he come here a lot?"

65

"Yes, but played the tables. High stake poker, I think. Too rich for my blood."

"What kind of a man was he?"

"Arrogant. Got thrown out of the poker room on more than one occasion." She motioned her head to where a big neon sign blinked Poker. "They always let him come back. Never did understand that."

"Is there someone here he might have borrowed money from?"

"Shh. Not so loud. Yes, there is a woman here who does that sort of thing, but everyone pretends she doesn't."

A woman? I hadn't considered the possibility of a female murderer in this case. "Is she here now?"

"She's always here. She stays at a table in the restaurant. Dark hair, blue eyes, dressed to kill. I wouldn't take out a loan from her if I were you." The woman bolted to her feet and left as if sitting next to me was now a dangerous thing.

Spying an empty seat by the machines Mom and Shar played on, I switched seats, sitting between them. "Jennings played a lot of poker. Might have borrowed money from a loan shark. A woman."

"Really?" Shar frowned. "Didn't see that coming. Jennings was a big man. Would've been difficult for a man to shove under that table, much less a woman."

"What now?" Mom asked. "It isn't as if we can take out a loan. Don't they charge like a crazy-high interest rate? We'd lose a lot of money paying it back."

I drummed my fingers on the machine. "There has to be a way to question the woman without getting ourselves in trouble."

"Ma'am." One of the security guards tapped me on the shoulder. "Come with me, please."

My heart lodged in my throat. "What did I do?" Other than lose a few bucks?

"Come with me." His expression told me absolutely nothing as to why he wanted me to follow him. When Mom started to stand, he shook his head. "Just her."

My legs trembled as I rose to my feet. The guard wrapped his beefy hand around my arm and marched me away.

I glanced over my shoulder, eyes wide, to where Mom and Shar stared after us. Then, in sync, they followed, staying back a bit. I should have known they'd never let me be taken somewhere without them.

The guard guided me into the restaurant and a corner booth where a dark-haired woman sat. "Thank you, Willy." She folded her hands and sent me a sharp look. "Have a seat, please."

I slid into the booth, the vinyl creaking under me, and I was grateful to see Mom and Shar slip into the restaurant. They motioned to the hostess that they wanted the booth next to us. The hostess seemed to argue for a minute, then relented.

"Who are you?" I asked, trying not to let my worry show.

"I think you have an idea or you wouldn't have been asking questions." She sat back. "Are the two women who just entered with you?"

"Yes."

"Did you tell them of your curiosity about me?"

"Yes." Oh, no. What have I done?

She sighed. "Tell them to join us."

"Come on over." I scooted to make room. "Are you going to tell me your name?"

"I don't think so. People around here call me Queen. That's all you need to know. I do not want to know your name either. No links between us."

"Did Jennings owe you a lot of money?"

"Of course, he did. The man had no luck at gambling."

"Did you kill him?" Shar blurted.

"Don't be silly. I'd never recoup my money that way, now would I?"

"Any idea who might have?" Mom leaned forward.

"Tell me about his death."

I explained about the wedding, the earrings, and how he'd been stuffed under the buffet table. As I talked, some of the trepidation over sitting across from the woman trickled away. She didn't seem to have a problem with us, other than I'd asked some questions.

"It's safe to assume he'd resorted to stealing in order to pay me back. The poker room wouldn't allow him to play any longer since he owed money, and I wouldn't loan him more." She steepled her fingers under her chin. "You seem like a bright woman. What do you think is going on?"

I told her about Bill and Ted.

"Why aren't you focusing on those two?"

"There's nothing to suggest they killed Jennings," Shar said. "Stealing, yes, but murder…"

Queen snapped her fingers. When the hostess

came over, she asked what we wanted to drink and ordered chef salads for each of us, then for the hostess to send Willy over. "While we eat, I can give you some information on those two men. I have resources."

I bet she did. When I woke up this morning, I had no idea I'd be sitting across the table from a loan shark who wanted to help us—no names exchanged.

The security guard arrived within minutes. Queen gave him the name of the plumbing company and the two men. "I want everything you can find on them ASAP. Full names, addresses, family, friends, etc. Then print it all out for these ladies." She offered a thin smile in our direction. "You'll soon know whether those two are capable of murder."

The largest salad I'd ever seen was soon placed in front of each of us, along with our drink of choice. Queen sipped a glass of wine while the rest of us had tea.

"What got you into the loaning business?" Shar asked, stabbing a piece of hard-boiled egg with her fork.

"Lots of money and too much time."

"I bet you're capable of murder."

I widened my eyes and elbowed my friend. "Put a filter on."

"You do tend to say whatever is on your mind, don't you?" Queen's brows rose. "That could get you into trouble."

"Well?" Shar persisted.

"Am I capable of murder?" She shrugged. "I

think anyone is capable under the right circumstances, even you."

I tapped my foot under the table. Yes, this day could really turn out to be a winner, but why couldn't we wait for the information on Bill and Ted by playing the slots? I picked at my salad.

"Which one of you is the leader of this little group of gumshoes?" Queen glanced from one of us to the other.

"She is." Shar and Mom pointed at me.

"Someone has to be the sane one." I reached for my tea. "As you've probably noticed, this one tends to run off half-cocked." So many times, I almost called Shar by her name. Since I didn't want to know what would happen if we moved past anonymity, I checked myself.

Lunch turned out to be over an hour long. Finally, Willy returned with a folder. He slapped it on the table in front of me and strode away. Before leaving the restaurant, he turned with a scowl on his face. Even though his gaze locked on Queen, I flinched at the hatred radiating there.

"There you go, ladies. Now, if you'll take the file and go, I can move on with my day. I've appointments to keep."

Efficiently dismissed, we slid from the booth. "Thank you," I said.

"Oh, and please refrain from discussing me with anyone." Queen gave a cold smile. "I might not be so lenient next time."

I couldn't get out of there fast enough. Outside the restaurant, I slipped the folder into Mom's purse. "That went better than expected."

"Shar and I were worried when that brute of a guard took you away."

"The very brute you wanted me to flirt with?" I smirked.

"Well, that was before I knew he worked for a loan shark. A very cold-blooded one, I think."

"Shh." I grabbed her arm. "No talking about her while we're here." I glanced behind us. "Things could have gone much differently. Let's not push the issue."

"Come on. I'll teach you how to play roulette." Shar led us to a table, explained what the black and red squares were for, and where to place our "coins."

"This looks easy enough." I motioned for a server to bring me a diet soda.

"You should've used the machine on the wall," Mom said. "Now, you'll have to tip her."

"Oh, right." I dug a dollar bill from my pocket, then placed my bets. "I won two dollars!"

"Time for retirement." Shar laughed.

"I'm just here to have fun, not lose my tee-shirt." I also couldn't wait to dig into the pages in that folder. This could be the shortest mystery the three of us had ever solved. McIlroy would be happy. Justice would be served for the gambling Mr. Jennings.

Willy paced by our table too many times for comfort. His presence definitely took away the enjoyment of watching the roulette wheel spin.

"I'm ready to go. Let's find a place to spread out our notes away from prying eyes." I stood.

"No way." Shar pulled me back down. "Ignore

the guard and have fun. We don't get to just have fun much. Forget about finding a murderer. We're three gals out for an afternoon of fun."

"After talking to a killer loan shark," Mom whispered, casting Willy a glance. "But, I'm not ready to leave yet."

"Don't come crying to me if you get yourselves in trouble." I placed my next bet.

Chapter Nine

Brad met us at my apartment where we had spread Queen's information across my kitchen table. "You got these from a loan shark who didn't give you her name and didn't want yours?" His brow furrowed. "Why would she help you?"

"Feeling nice?" I shrugged. "Bill's last name is Roberts, Ted's is Olson. They've worked for Waterfall Plumbing for a little less than three years, having been hired around the same time." I reached for my glass of tea. "I don't remember a rash of crime around that time, do you?" I glanced around the group.

"There's been a lot of crime the last year or so," Shar said. "Ever since big business moved in." She cut a sideways look at Brad.

"Hey, it's not my fault my father saw potential here." He frowned. "I'm doing my best to improve this city. If I were to shut everything down, lots of people would be out of a job."

"I'm not accusing you, just stating a fact." She tapped the page in front of her. "They attend

Waterfall Community. That's a pretty upscale church."

"Probably scouting out victims," Mom said. "That's where Joe and I go, and I've never seen them. Just because they're on the member list, doesn't mean they actually attend."

"It might make some look the other way to them being suspects." Maybe. Sounded far-fetched to me. "They could attend a different service than you and Dad."

"Sure, they could. We like the earlier one. I bet they go to the second service. We'll check it out this Sunday."

Brad reached over and grabbed one of the copies. "Both spent time in juvie for theft. How did this Queen find all this out in an hour? She's going to want something in return, ladies. People like her don't help out of the kindness of their heart."

"She didn't say she wanted anything." What could we possibly have that she wanted? "Maybe she just wanted us to stop asking questions."

Brad didn't appear convinced. "Loan sharks are dangerous people."

"You sound like you know from first-hand experience."

"Thankfully, I do not. Oh, goody. Ted was arrested for aggravated assault. How did these two get hired anywhere?"

Mom rattled a page. "Because the owner is Ted's cousin. Turning a blind eye is my guess. This still doesn't mean they're killers."

"Unless it was an argument that got out of hand." I exhaled heavily and leaned back in my chair. "I'm too tired to think anymore tonight. We'll decide our next step tomorrow. Let's meet somewhere after you come home from church."

"Come to our house." Mom stood and collected her purse. "I'll make a roast. You, too, Shar. Bring the detective if he's available. I'll let you know if we see our thieves at the service."

After everyone left and Brad kissed me goodnight, I stumbled into bed, surrounded by one massive dog and two cats. I fell asleep in the tiny space on the mattress left to me and dreamed of loan sharks.

Brad picked me up bright and early the next morning with fresh bagels and coffee. "Ready to see our house?"

"Absolutely." I opened the bag of bagels and drew in a deep breath. "I guess we should tell my parents at dinner that we've set our date."

"Your mom is going to freak at the length of time she has to prepare."

"I want something small. Is that all right?"

He leaned over and kissed me. "Sounds perfect." Then he straightened and started the car. "You're trying to find out who killed Jennings is going to cut into the wedding planning big time."

True. I'd have to do some clever time management.

Brad pulled onto a curving gravel drive lined with crepe myrtle. They'd be beautiful in bloom. At the end of the drive stood what had once been a beautiful Victorian-style home. The gray paint and white trim badly needed repair. Some of the gingerbread trim had broken off. A few of the fish-scale shingles had fallen. A turret I'd already claimed as a library rose above the house. Despite the disrepair, I could see how it would look when Brad and I finished renovating it.

I ran my hand over the porch railing as Sheba explored. "We'll be living in the penthouse for quite a while."

"A year, maybe less." He held out his hand.

I slipped mine in his and he led me to the front door. To my surprise the stained glass insert remained unshattered. This filled me with hope that we really could restore this lovely lady to her previous splendor.

We stepped onto dusty oak floors. A winding staircase led to the second floor. To our right, a parlor with a stone fireplace. To our left, a dining room that led to the kitchen. Brad led me to the left.

"The kitchen isn't workable right now, but it will be a chef's dream. I thought we could have it renovated first, then the bathrooms. That way, we could move in while the rest of the work is being done and start the farm you want so much." His eyes begged me to agree.

"That's a great idea." I loved the house. I really did. What bothered me was that he'd bought it without consulting me. We hadn't gone together to look at houses. That's the part of losing my independence I worried about—why it had taken me so long to set a date. Not because I didn't love Brad, but because we're both so used to doing what we want when we want that we sometimes leave out the other person.

"What's wrong?" Brad peered into my eyes.

"It's going to be beautiful."

"But?"

My shoulders slumped. "I wanted to go house hunting together when it was time."

He took both my hands in his. "I'm sorry. This house was such a steal that I didn't want it to be sold before you could see it. I can sell it. We can start looking again."

"Don't be silly. I'm being truthful when I say I love it. Let's just try not to do any big things without the other from now on, okay?"

"Promise." He tapped me on the nose with his finger. "That also means you always tell me where you're going when you're snooping." He must have noticed my irritation because he quickly added, "Only when snooping. You don't have to tell me every time you go to the store or a friend's house. I doubt anyone will try to kill you there. But, otherwise, I need to know. Most of the time, I can probably go with you. If you want me to."

I smiled. "Are you auditioning to be a Waterfall Sleuth?"

"No, just a concerned husband."

"I can agree to those terms. Plus, don't forget we have trackers on each of our phones. Now, show me the rest of the house."

Four bedrooms, four baths, a study, a master as big as my apartment. The turret was as glorious as I'd imagined. Definitely the library. "This will be my most favorite room in the house. Every available wall space will be filled with books. Cozy chairs will provide a place to read or have a conversation. And look at that view." I stepped to one of the windows. The acreage stretched behind the house with meadows and a pond.

I could already envision chickens, goats, a few cows... "It's absolutely perfect."

"Let's check out our room." He led me back to the second floor.

A large, four-poster bed took up the space between two windows. With some polish and elbow grease and a new mattress it would be perfect. Except for the antique doll hanging by a bit of yarn around its neck.

The doll's faded yellow dress blended in with the wallpaper. Sightless eyes stared straight at me. "That is the most hideous thing I've ever seen."

"Almost as bad as this painting."

I spun to see an oil painting of a fawn lying in a patch of wildflowers. The fawn was supposed to be looking over its shoulder, but the way it was painted, it looked as if the head was on backward. Creepy. "Let's remove these two things."

"I'll put them in the trunk of my car while you keep looking around." Brad gathered the two items and headed down the stairs.

By the time I joined him, dinnertime was fast approaching. Brad exited the kitchen, a tape measure in his hand. "I'm starving."

My stomach growled in response. "Me too. Mom makes a good roast."

"Looks like I didn't close my trunk all the way." Brad jumped off the porch and headed for his car.

I called for Sheba who came trotting around the corner of the house, grass stuck in her hair and dirt on her nose. "What have you been into?" The dogs would love this place.

"The painting and the doll are missing." Brad stared into his trunk.

"Maybe you put them in the back seat."

"No, I put them here." He backed up and scanned the property. "I wouldn't think there would be anyone way out here to play such tricks."

I shrugged. "There have to be neighbors."

"Half a mile away is the closest."

"Probably kids. No loss." I opened the door for Sheba to jump into the back seat.

"You're right. I'm reading too much into a couple of missing creepy items. Let's go eat."

We arrived at Mom's and Dad's small ranch home twenty minutes later. Their Corgi, Honey, immediately wanted to play with Sheba who plopped on the floor with a huff. The cat, Prince, hissed and darted under the sofa.

"Smells good." I gave Mom a hug. "What do you want me to help with?"

"Shar is already in the kitchen. Brad, why don't you join the men in the living room. Dinner is almost ready."

"I'm making gravy." Shar held up a dripping spoon. "Can't have a roast with carrots and potatoes without gravy."

Reaching into the cupboard, I counted out six plates and set the table. I couldn't wait to tell my family and friends about the wedding date and the house.

While we ate, I asked about Bill and Ted. "Were they at church?"

"No," Dad said. "We asked if they were regular

attendees, and one of the deacons said they were, up until a couple of weeks ago. Haven't shown up at any of the services since. Joined the church and stopped coming."

"Putting up a pretense?" Why go to the trouble?

"Maybe."

Right before dessert, I clinked my fork on my water glass. Nothing fancy, just the type in most kitchens. Everyone stopped chatting and looked at me. "Brad and I have an announcement." I grinned. "Today, we looked at the fixer-upper he bought us. A Victorian about ten miles outside of town. Why did he buy us a house, you ask?" My grin widened. "We've set our wedding date. It's June fifth."

"That's awesome," Mom said. "That gives us a year to prepare."

"This June fifth."

She frowned. "How do you propose we plan a wedding and catch a killer in about six weeks?"

"I know." Shar jumped to her feet. "We'll make it a double wedding. Alex and I will get married at the same time. That way, we can split the planning right down the middle."

The coffeepot in Alex's hand overflowed his cup.

Brad sputtered in protest.

Mom's eyes widened to the point I thought they'd pop out of her head.

Welcome to my world. "Oh, and Brad and I found a creepy doll hanging in the house. I asked him to take it out, and someone stole it out of his trunk at the house, along with a very bad painting."

Everyone started talking at once.

Honey barked.

Sheba raised an ear.

I laughed, shrugged, and dug my fork into the strawberry cheesecake in front of me. I'd sort it all out tomorrow.

Chapter Ten

Text messages flooded my phone the next morning. Mom, frantic at the lack of time to plan a wedding to her satisfaction. Brad, irritated at having to share a ceremony with crazy Shar. Alex, worried about the doll disappearing from the trunk. And Dad, overjoyed at our announcement. He ended his message with, "Let's do it again soon."

I laughed and got up to feed my pets. No, I didn't want to share a wedding with Shar. We had plenty of time for a simple wedding, and it did strike me as strange that the doll and painting had been taken. After I fed the dog and cats, I responded to the texts, then took a shower.

With a spring in my step, I skipped down the stairs to the shop. I unlocked the door, flipped the sign to open, turned toward my desk, and froze. Staring at me with beady, painted eyes was the creepy doll.

Ha. Brad must have been joking yesterday and saw an opportunity to pull a prank. Well, if that's what he wanted, I'd pull one back on him. I dropped the doll into a bag, then shoved it in the cabinet until I could hide it in his apartment.

"Why don't you want to have a double ceremony?" Shar marched into the store. "Cheaper and we can divvy up the planning."

"I want my own day. Besides, did Alex even propose to you?" From the look on his face yesterday, her announcement had been a big surprise.

"After we got home last night." She grinned, putting her purse in the cupboard. "I guess my blurting out had him taking the much needed step."

"Not nice, Shar." I wiggled my finger at her. "You shouldn't coerce a man into marrying you."

"We'd talked about it, just nothing definite." Undeterred from her wrongdoing, she moved to the grooming room.

As soon as Heather entered, I said, "We set the date for June fifth." I didn't want her to feel left out.

"It's about time." She smiled. "You've kept Brad waiting long enough."

"We only met last year." Marriage isn't the only goal in life for a successful businesswoman. "Some people are engaged for several years."

"Not around here. You grew up here. All we talked about as kids was getting married and having babies. At least your mom will be off your back."

"No, now she'll hound me about babies." I booted up my computer as Brad entered the shop carrying our coffees. "Good morning." He looked all innocent after leaving that ugly doll.

"Hey, gorgeous." His gaze flicked through the window to where Shar readied the grooming room.

"Thanks for not wanting to share a wedding with her."

"Shar wanted to have a double wedding?" Heather's eyes widened. "Obviously, I'm the last to know the news."

"Sorry. We made the announcement yesterday at my parents' house. I would like you to be my matron of honor."

Her eyes widened. "I'm honored." She smiled and thanked Brad for her drink.

After Brad headed across the street to his office in the theater, I filled Heather in on the house. "It's going to be beautiful."

"Sounds like a lot of work to me. Brad could have built you the perfect house."

"He fell in love with this one. I did, too, after seeing it." I went on to tell her about the doll and the painting. "People leave behind the strangest things when they move. I wonder who owned the house before Brad bought it?"

"The Carsons. He had health problems, so they moved into assisted living six months ago. At least, I think that's the house you're talking about. It's over a hundred years old. People say it's haunted. Maybe the ghosts took the doll."

Well, I knew that wasn't true. "I don't believe in ghosts."

"Neither do I, but kids out riding around have seen strange lights in the windows."

"Why would kids be way out there?"

She shrugged. "What do you want me to do today?"

"Inventory? That way I'll know what we need to

order." I turned my attention to my emails, noting several reservations for boarding and one for someone looking for a miniature dachshund puppy to buy. That would be harder, but I knew of breeders I could check with.

By lunchtime, our kennels were full, and I'd located a puppy. "I'll be back in a bit. Need to run something by Brad's place." I grabbed the bag with the doll and headed to my SUV, Sheba on my heels.

More than a few times, I glanced in my rearview mirror. Was that a dark sedan following me? No, it turned off on the road before my turn. Simply two people headed in the same direction. In the past when I'd been followed, the one behind me hadn't cared about me knowing they were there.

I'd definitely have to tell Brad about our house being haunted. I pulled into the parking garage of his building and used the elevator to take me to the penthouse floor. After punching in the code to unlock the front door, I stepped inside and looked around. Where would be the best place to hide the doll in order to startle him the most?

The shower. I'd hang her from the shower head. Brad always took a shower before bed and wouldn't suspect a thing. Giddy from pulling the prank, I grabbed the fixings of a sandwich from his fridge and rushed back to my vehicle. I'd eat on the way back to work.

Spiders skittered down my back as I spotted a dark sedan behind me again. When had it pulled behind me? There were a lot of dark sedans around, right? My past had taught me not to believe in coincidences.

I took a roundabout way back to the store. Yep, the car was tailing me. I pulled in front of the store instead of parking in back as I usually did. The car passed as I slid out of my SUV and let Sheba out of the back seat. The license plates were splattered with mud making them illegible.

"Come on, girl. Getting the plate number would've been too easy."

"What's wrong?" Heather glanced over when I entered. "You look upset."

"I think someone followed me as I was out driving."

"Are you sure?" She frowned. "Maybe you should call the detective."

"They didn't do anything. Didn't try running me off the road. Just followed me. Maybe it was one of the loan shark's goons."

"You should never have sat down with that woman."

"I didn't really have a choice." I stowed my bag back in the cupboard. "The guard escorted me." The more I thought about it, the stranger it all became. Why would a loan shark want to help me bring down a murderer and a couple of thieves? Things went far deeper than I thought. "I can't call McIlroy on nothing more than an assumption."

"Okay, but be careful."

"I plan on it."

"What's the next move in finding Mr. Jennings' killer?"

I sat behind the counter. "I'm not sure. It's almost as if we have two cases here. The murder and the thefts. But, Mr. Jennings did have your earrings in his possession when he died, so the two might be connected. I'm thinking I might need some plumbing done. The problem is...I don't have anything worth stealing." Except my engagement ring, and I'd never risk that precious item. "I've some thinking to do."

Brad picked me up after work to take back to his place. He liked cooking and enjoyed fixing supper for the two of us. "Let me shower real quick, then I'll start these steaks."

"Sure thing." I grinned, resisting the urge to rub my hands together.

A few seconds later, Brad yelped, then returned to the living room where I grinned like a sneaky cat. "That doll is in my shower."

"Scared you, didn't it?"

His eyes narrowed. "How did it get there?"

Confused at his confusion, did I detect a hint of anger? "I put it there because you put it in my store this morning."

"No, I didn't." He gripped my shoulders. "What do you mean it was in your store?"

"Sitting on the counter when I went down. I thought you were playing a trick on me, so I did the same."

"Trin, I didn't put that doll there. Whoever took it out of my trunk was in your store. I'm calling McIlroy."

"Someone followed me when I came here to hide the doll." I sagged onto his soft-as-butter leather sofa. "They didn't try to run me off the road or anything. Just followed me here, then back to the store."

His features darkened as he called McIlroy. "I need you to come to the penthouse as soon as possible." He listened for a minute, then hung up. "He said he'll be here in ten minutes." Brad sat next to me and took my hands in his. "I'm getting worried. Usually, someone is making threats to you by now, not this sneaking-around stuff."

He was right. Usually, I'd received an in-your-face, keep-your-nose-out-of-things note by now. "I haven't really been out there asking questions."

"Maybe not, but someone knows you're going to." He sprang up at the knock on the door. After looking through the peephole, he let McIlroy in. "In the bathroom."

"Okay." The detective shot me a curious look but followed Brad.

They returned a few minutes later. McIlroy recited to us that I'd found the doll, thought Brad was pulling a prank, then decided to retaliate. "And someone followed you. Am I correct?"

"That sums it up." I slumped against the cushions. "Oh, and I talked to a loan shark the other day at the casino who strangely enough wants to or appears to want to help me find out who killed Mr. Jennings. In a surprisingly short time, an hour actually, she dug up a lot of info on Bill Roberts and Ted Olson. Both plumbers at Waterfall Plumbing. Oh, and I heard our new house is haunted."

McIlroy looked as if his head was going to explode. If his face got any redder, I feared he might have a stroke. "I'll need that information. Do you have any idea who you're dealing with? The Loan Queen is toying with you. You're her new favorite pastime. When she tires of you, she'll dispose of you."

"Why me?" My blood chilled.

"She wants to know who you're looking for, knows you usually figure out the puzzle, and she'll most likely entice them to work for her. The Queen likes knowing who isn't afraid of killing."

"Then why isn't she behind bars?" I crossed my arms. "If she's so bad, why haven't you arrested her?"

"Because the evidence is all circumstantial. We haven't been able to gather anything concrete against her." He lowered into an armchair. "This got real bad in a hurry. As usual, it's time for Trinity to stay here with you, Brad. I'll assign Officer Snowe as protection outside. She'll follow Trinity to work each day."

"Absolutely not. I won't be able to do any investigating with her dogging my steps. The sooner this is all tied up, the sooner the loan shark is off my back."

"If your snooping digs up the dirt we need on her, you're toast." McIlroy stood. "As in a very, very burnt piece of bread."

Chapter Eleven

The next morning, I explained last night's events to my mother and friends as we enjoyed our morning coffee. "So, I'm back to staying at Brad's."

"Queen didn't seem that bad to me." Mom shook her head. "Just a woman making a living by loaning money at a high interest rate. Although,"—she held up a finger, "Queen never did deny whether she'd ever killed someone."

"Forget her," Shar said. "I want to check out the haunted house. Let's go tonight."

"I don't believe in ghosts." I flipped through wedding photos of Mom and Dad that I had uploaded years ago. "May I wear your wedding dress, Mom?"

"You're smaller than me."

"I'll have it tailored." One item checked off my list. The more I looked at the 1960s simple satin gown, the more I loved it. The dress rested on the tip of the shoulders and skimmed the hips, falling to a short train. "We'll have the wedding at the lake like Heather did." Second item checked off the list.

"Reception will be at the new house." Check number three. I'm sure Brad could finish renovating one of the bathrooms by then. Now, all I needed was to choose a caterer and bridesmaid dresses. Vintage bridesmaid dresses. I found the cutest knee-length, full-skirted gowns in baby blue, ordered one in both Shar's and Heather's sizes, and scooted back my chair. "All I need now is a caterer."

"We're discussing how to dispel the rumor that your house is haunted." Shar narrowed her eyes. "Aren't you listening?"

"Yes. Fine. We'll go after work." I felt rather pleased with how quickly I ticked off most of the items on my wedding list. Oh, wait, I'd need flowers.

"It has to be dark, Trinity." Exasperation laced Shar's voice. "Ghosts come out at night. Even fake ones."

I sighed. "Okay, but I hope y'all don't mind a bit of dirt. And, while the bathroom works, it's not pretty."

"Water and electricity?" Mom asked.

I nodded. "All turned on. Brad wants to start renovating this weekend." We weren't kids. Why spend time in a dilapidated house? I turned my attention back to the computer and looked up the website for our local florist. Fifteen minutes later, I'd ordered bouquets, corsages, centerpieces, and decorations. Then, I went to a site to order a tent and table and chairs, before starting to design the invitations.

"She isn't listening again," Shar complained.

"What?" I glanced up. "If you're planning on

getting married in June, you'd better start planning, too."

"We changed our date to August. If things become interesting tonight, plan on spending it in the house. Bring bedding."

I had a bed. Sure, it had an old mattress, but the master bedroom was furnished. "I'm pretty sure Brad and McIlroy will blow a gasket about us spending the night out there. Especially now that they're worried about Queen."

"Then ask them to come along. The more the merrier."

"No ghosts will show if there are a lot of people, Shar." Mom patted her shoulder. "You're as giddy as a kid. This all needs to be hush-hush."

"The men will never let us go alone." I reached for my melting frozen coffee.

"Just tell them we're going to have our bachelorette party out there tonight with games, ideas for decorating, and wedding planning." My conniving mother smiled. "Girl stuff. They won't be interested and, since no one outside of our circle will know we're there, they'll say okay."

"Why is this so important? Don't we have other things to do? Like finding out who killed Mr. Jennings?" I arched a brow.

"What if they're connected? Focus on the doll." She tapped her nails on the table. "It hung in the house. Someone took it out of Brad's trunk. You found it again here. I'm telling you it's connected."

"So, Brad just happened to buy a house connected with our investigation?" Too contrived.

"Stranger things have happened. Especially

around you."

Unfortunately, true. Now, my mind careened onto the same path as theirs. "What if the thieves are using my house to hide their bounty? It sat vacant for months, and you can't see the neighbors."

"We should bring a hammer and a crowbar," Shar said. "Start pulling up boards."

"No way are you going to rip up that house." I glared. "The floors are original and in good shape. If you don't find a loose board, you leave it alone, or I'll use the crowbar on you."

"Don't get yourself in a tizzy. I promise not to destroy anything. Ah, there's my first appointment." She stood and greeted a woman with a wriggling poodle in her arms.

"I'd best go to work. See you at eight o'clock tonight. We'll meet at my house. Less conspicuous than here." Mom hugged me and waltzed out the door.

I sent Brad a text about the night's plans and asked what kind of food he wanted at the wedding. He responded that he would take care of the catering and that I was to call him every hour while at the house. If I didn't call, he'd be there with McIlroy in tow.

That I could do. At least there'd be no argument about me going. Mom was right. Men weren't interested in womanly things. Plus, I wouldn't be alone and each of us women carried a gun in our bag.

The rest of the day passed as usual. I placed a supply order off the inventory list Heather had done the day before, then fed and watered the daycare and boarding animals before letting them out in the run to play for a while. At the end of the workday, I closed the store and headed to my apartment to pack an overnight bag with clothes and snacks.

"Well, baby girl. It appears we're spending the night at the house with a couple of crazies on the hunt for a ghost."

Sheba's ears perked up.

"We might encounter danger if the so-called ghost is actually alive and breathing, but I'm sure we can handle Bill and Ted." Had one of them stolen the doll and the painting? Where was the painting? I shrugged. "We'll find our answers in time. We always do." While I still thought it a far stretch that the alleged ghost in my house was somehow connected to Jennings, I'd play along. A sleepover with Mom and Shar might be fun.

Since Shar would meet us at my parents' house, I loaded Sheba and my things into the SUV and drove over there for supper. I texted Brad where I was going, keeping my promise to start contacting him every hour.

Mom served burritos made with the leftover pot roast. "I'm really excited about tonight. My gut tells me we're going to learn something important."

"Yeah, like what a harebrained idea it is," Dad said, slathering his burrito with hot sauce. "Keep your guns handy."

"We'll be fine. No one knows we're going." Mon patted his shoulder on the way to her seat. "Besides, we'll have three dogs to alert us if anyone is around."

"That makes me feel better. Shar's pooch yaps at anything. Trouble shows up, call the police immediately, then the rest of us." His sharp gaze landed on Mom, then me. "I'm serious."

"Yes, dear." Mom bit into her burrito.

Shar showed up right on time. Since we had the three dogs, I drove to the property. A moonless night and no streetlights left the place in utter darkness. I grabbed a flashlight from the glove box and called for Sheba to follow me. "Y'all wait until I've put some lights on."

Utter silence matched the pitch-black darkness. If not for Sheba at my side, I'd have turned back to the car and not gone into the house. It took some fumbling before I had the key in the lock. The door opened and I reached in, sliding my hand along the wall where I thought I'd seen a light switch when I'd been there with Brad.

There. I flipped it up. A light flickered to life over my head. "Okay. Y'all can come in now."

"This will be nice when it's fixed up," Mom said, glancing into the parlor. "Oh, look. A ratty old sofa. I'll sleep there."

"I'm upstairs in the master bedroom." I headed for the stairs.

"Alone? In this haunted house?" Her eyes widened.

"Well, now that you mention it." It would be scary up there all alone. "I have Sheba."

"Right. Shar?" Mom glanced her way.

"I'll bunk in here with you. That recliner will suit me fine."

Neither piece of furniture looked comfortable to

me, but it would be better than the floor. With Sheba on my heels, I headed to the master bedroom, turning on every light I passed. Most of the bulbs were burned out, but those that worked gave me enough light to see.

I quickly made the bed with clean sheets and a blanket, then made sure the toilet flushed in the master bath. It did, and I could live with the pink bathroom for a while.

A thud sounded down the hall.

Sheba's ears pricked up.

"Hello?"

"Hello?" Mom parroted from downstairs.

I must be hearing things. Old houses made noise while settling, right? "Come on, Sheba. Let's head downstairs."

"Turn off the lights as you come," Mom called. "Ghosts don't like lights. I brought some candles."

"If there is anyone here other than us, they're alive and mean us no good," I said entering the living room/parlor. "I'd rather see trouble coming."

Starr and Honey both raced to the front door barking loud enough to wake the dead. Ew. I glanced at Sheba who stared at the door as if she could see through the wood.

I rushed forward and threw the deadbolt. How could I have forgotten to lock the doors? With flashlight on, I whispered loudly, "I need to check the back door. One of you check the bottom windows."

"Do you really think someone is out there?" Shar jumped to her feet.

"The dogs think so. Could be a critter, but I'm

not taking any chances." I crept toward the kitchen, swinging my light back and forth.

"We should have brought Prince," Mom said. "Cats can see ghosts."

My eyes rolled. "There's no such thing as ghosts." I felt like a broken record.

The dogs settled down as I turned the lock on the kitchen door. I peered out the faded yellow and white striped curtains. Nothing moved in the darkness that I could see. The curtains fell back into place and I rejoined the others.

Scooching between them, I pulled up the pictures of the dress I wanted my bridesmaids to wear. "Isn't this cute?"

"Reminds me of my mother's prom dress," Shar said. "Why are you going old-fashioned? I'm going to go modern and glittery."

"I'm not a glittery type of gal." I moved to the floor, using Sheba as a backrest. "Brad is taking care of the food, so we're all set once I send out invitations."

"You don't have time for people to RSVP." Mom frowned.

"It's going to be small. Not more than fifty people."

"I always wanted you to have a big wedding with all the fanfare." She pouted. "But, at least you're getting married. Now, I can start hoping for grandkids."

I groaned. "Give me a few years, please."

"You're twenty-eight!"

"I have plenty of time." I stretched out my legs and crossed my ankles. I did want kids, just not right away.

Another thud from upstairs.

Sheba took off from under me so suddenly that I fell back, hitting my head on the floor.

The other two dogs yapped and gave chase.

Sheba's deep growl drifted down the stairs.

"I don't think we're alone in the house," I said. "Call the police."

Chapter Twelve

"Not until we make sure it isn't a raccoon," Shar said heading for the stairs, gun in hand. "We wouldn't want to appear foolish like those senseless women who call a man at the slightest noise."

No, we wouldn't want that. "Right. Let's be those too-stupid-to-live girls in a B-rated horror movie." I strained to hear past the noise of the dogs barking. When I couldn't detect anything that sounded like a human footstep, it was easier to believe maybe a raccoon *had* gotten in as Shar believed.

Huddled together, the three of us climbed the stairs. I stepped on a step that creaked, and we froze. When nothing jumped out at us, we continued to the top and turned left. The dogs barked in front of a door I knew led to the attic. I turned the knob.

"Be careful," Mom hissed. "It might have rabies."

"We don't know what it is yet. Quiet your dogs." I put a finger to my lips, then my hand on Sheba's head. "Or, better yet, take your dogs downstairs. Sheba and I can handle this." I hoped.

My heart threatened to beat free as I climbed the narrow, dark stairs.

"Psst."

I glanced back to see Shar holding out her gun to me. "I have mine in my waistband."

"Then take it out."

She frowned and scooped up Starr. "See you downstairs." The coward turned and followed my mother.

Taking shallow breaths, I continued my climb. Some of the tension in Sheba resurfaced. She glanced upward. "Did it go to the roof, girl?" Definitely a critter.

Something banged from the other side of the attic. I jumped and stifled a shriek. Further investigation revealed an unlatched window. I giggled at my jumpiness and secured the latch. "Nothing more to see here."

With one more glance at the roof, Sheba padded after me. I shut the attic door securely and joined the others. "A window wasn't closed all the way. Whatever was in the attic is gone now."

"See how silly we would've looked if we'd called the police?" Shar leaned back in the recliner and pulled a blanket to her chin. "No wonder it was chilly. How many more windows are open?"

We returned to chat about our normal subjects—weddings, loan sharks, murder. I pulled up local news on my phone to see whether anything else had been stolen. "A painting was taken out of the country club. Worth thousands."

"How in the world did anyone do that? It

would've had to be after hours, right?" Mom's brow furrowed. "The place is always packed until it closes."

"The article says someone pulled the fire alarm. Once everything settled back down, the painting was gone."

"Bill and Ted don't seem the country-club type," Shar said, fiddling with Starr's ears. "You can't get in unless you're a member or with a member."

"Which means we need to find that out." I shut off my phone. "I'm about ready for—" Sheba's dash for the door cut me off mid-sentence. "If there's a critter out there again, I'm going to shoot it." Gun in hand, I ordered Sheba to stay back and yanked the front door open, feeling very much like a tough girl from an action movie.

The darkness consumed me. It took a few seconds for my eyes to adjust. When they did, nothing moved other than the breeze through the willow oaks and crepe myrtles. I took another step, pulling the door partially closed behind me to keep the dogs in. If one of the rowdy ones ran out, we'd have a dickens of a time finding them if they chose to hide.

The rustle of a nearby bush had me holding my breath. I cleared my throat. "Get out of there. Shoo." I looked for something to throw. Not even a rock on the porch offered help. My phone vibrated. Brad—whoops, I forgot to text him. I sent him a quick message that I was chasing a varmint out of the house and would be going to bed.

He responded goodnight and he loved me. I said

ditto, then put my phone back in my pocket and resumed my search for an animal that wouldn't go away.

A light flickered on upstairs. I stepped into the yard and peered upward. A light shone in one of the upstairs bedrooms. This house really had some issues. It wasn't hard to figure out why people think it haunted. Banging windows, flickering lights, sneaky critters.

I turned back to the yard for one final look. Something moved from behind a tree. Something that stood on two legs and wore a white clown mask. Another stood from the bushes. I screamed and scrambled for the porch.

Losing my footing, I crawled up the stairs like a manic crab until I leapt into the house and kicked the door closed. "Call the police. We've got clowns." Oh, what if the light upstairs was because of a clown? "We need to lock ourselves away somewhere." My chest heaved. My heart dropped to my stomach.

"Clowns?" Mom peered out the window. "Oh, Lordy!" She dropped the curtains back into place and grabbed Honey. "Where can we hide? They know we're in here. Upstairs?"

"A light came on upstairs just seconds ago." I struggled to stand.

"Then we wait for the showdown." Shar tossed off her blanket and grabbed her gun from the end table. "I hate clowns. What are they doing now?"

I peeked through the small window in the door. "Standing there staring at the house. Call the police."

"Right." Shar punched in numbers on her phone. "Alex, we need you over here right now. We've got clowns in the front yard. Yes, you heard correctly. I don't think they're here for a party." She hung up. "He'll be here lickety-split." Shar moved to the door and bellowed, "I've called the police, and we all have guns!"

A bullet tore through the wall.

"So do they." I dropped to the floor.

Sheba lay next to me while the two smaller dogs dove under the sofa. My brave girl trembled in spite of her desire to stay with me.

Gunfire sprayed the house before stopping at the sound of a police siren. I crawled to the front door and peered out. Three clowns ran across the lawn and toward the back of the house. I darted for the kitchen door in time to see them sprint across the fields in back, melting into the darkness.

I then raced up the stairs to the room where I'd seen the light come on. The window hung open. Footprints in the dust led from the window to the closet and back again. The only varmints we'd been dealing with were of the two-legged variety. I went downstairs to talk to McIlroy.

Brad entered right behind him and made a beeline for me. He wrapped strong arms around me and released a heavy sigh. Not speaking, he simply held me until I stopped trembling.

"All right, ladies." McIlroy motioned to the sofa. "Officers Snowe and Rice will check out the house and outside while I ask some questions."

"The three clowns ran across the field in back." I sat on the sofa, while Brad perched on the arm.

The two officers raced out the backdoor.

"Trinity, start from the beginning."

I began with the noise upstairs while I put my things in the master bedroom and finished with shots being fired at the house. "We honestly thought it was a raccoon or a squirrel until we saw the clowns."

"Did they let on what they wanted?"

"In the house, apparently. At least one had been in the attic and another in one of the guest rooms." I shuddered knowing they'd been in the house with us. "They couldn't do much undetected because of the three dogs."

"Thank God," Brad muttered. "First time I've been grateful for yappers. At least they couldn't have reached you unnoticed."

I leaned against him, taking strength from his solidness. "Why clowns?"

"Jokesters." McIlroy muttered, his face set in hard lines. "This is the kind of game Queen plays."

"But why this house?"

"Everyone in town knows it stood vacant for six months." He didn't say it, but I knew he believed there could be something hidden here, and the clowns had been on the hunt. "Could you tell whether these people were male or female?"

"Not with certainty, but I believe they were male. One seemed large."

"Caucasian?"

I shrugged. "I couldn't tell."

"All right. Pack your things. The three of you are going home. Brad will follow and make sure each of you arrive home safely."

I decided to leave the bedding and grabbed my bag. I could collect the sheets when Brad and I came to do renovations.

The two officers had returned by the time I went back downstairs. The clowns had driven away in a dark panel van. No one could see the license plate in the dark. So much for answers.

Brad and McIlroy followed us to the SUV, then Brad climbed into his Mercedes. When he flashed his lights, I drove away from the house. Tears pricked my eyes.

"What's wrong?" Mom put a hand on my arm. "Are you crying?"

"Some of the joy is gone from that house now." I sniffed.

"Nonsense. So, you have a few more holes in the walls. Those can be fixed."

"I'm talking about the peace that three clowns ripped away." I cut her a sharp look.

"That too will pass once they're behind bars. Who knew that friendly Queen could be into games? You do know that if they'd wanted us dead, they'd have shot through the front door, right? That's where we hunkered down."

"I thought that woman wanted to help us," Shar said from the backseat. "What does she really want?"

"Money," I said. "She's behind the thefts." The idea hit me upside the head like a two-by-four. "All we have to do is prove it. Find the evidence against her that the police haven't found."

"How?" Mom asked.

"I don't know yet, but I'll think of something." I

tightened my grip on the steering wheel. Look out, Queen, the Waterfall Sleuths are good at what they do.

"Uh oh." Mom glanced over her shoulder at Shar. "My daughter has that look on her face that makes most people run in the opposite direction."

"Good. That's when things really start happening." Shar laughed.

Mom and I laughed with her, the tears drying in my eyes. Brad and I would make the house something to be proud of. I had our wedding planned. That left time to find out who our clowns were. I had my suspicions. Bill, Ted, and the big clown could easily be Willy, who definitely tied Queen to what had happened tonight.

Those goons might not have wanted to kill us, only scare us from the house, but a stray bullet could have hit one of us or one of the dogs. We couldn't stand for that.

I dropped Shar off first and waited while Brad escorted her to the front door, making sure it was locked. Then repeated the same thing with Mom, except Dad met her on the porch with a hug.

Brad followed me to the garage of his apartment complex and parked next to the SUV. After scanning the garage, he opened my door. "Let's get you upstairs and ready for bed. You look beat."

"I am. Beat, but determined."

"Uh oh. I recognize that look. Things just got serious."

"Yes, my love, they did." I gave him a quick kiss and marched to the elevator, my mind whirling. I'd bet Sheba's food dish that a visit to the casino would show Queen not at her usual table. My guess—the woman had moved onto newer hunting grounds. If she knew as much about me as she said she did, she'd know I suspected her by now. She'd also know one of my friends was marrying Detective McIlroy. Things had heated up for Queen.

Chapter Thirteen

I still didn't have a plan by the time we drove to the house that weekend. I sat on the top porch step, one arm around Sheba, and tapped my foot, staring at the places the clowns had appeared. My gaze drifted to where Brad strolled up, a tool belt hanging around his waist, and his dog Barney sniffing the ground behind him. He'd hired a crew to renovate the house but still wanted to do some of the work himself.

"I'm going to start on the master bath. Wanna help?" He stopped at the bottom of the steps.

"Might as well. I can patch the bullet holes in the siding." Sometimes, my brain put the pieces of a puzzle together with mindless work.

"That's my girl." He grinned and stepped past me, entering the house.

I took the spackling and tool off the porch rail and started filling holes. Those clowns hadn't wanted to kill us, only scare us away. Why? Because something was hidden in the house. I smiled and jumped off the porch to the yard and stared at the window with the light from the other night.

That room and the attic had been where one of them had gone hunting for something. But if they'd hidden whatever they were here for, wouldn't they have known where to find it?

I returned to patching holes. What if there'd been a double cross? My mind whirled with possibilities. If someone not part of the clown trio had come here and moved whatever the clowns had been searching for, they wouldn't know where to search. I needed to check for loose floorboards and paneling.

Finished with the few holes in the front wall of the house, I went inside and straight up the stairs to find Brad. "I'm going to look for whatever the clowns had been searching for in the attic."

He glanced up from removing the toilet. "A little help, first. Hold this black garbage bag so we can wrap it around the tank, then I'll need you to help me carry it outside."

"Gross, Brad." I gripped the bag. "I'm not interested in leaking toilet water on me."

"That's why I'm wearing gloves." He laughed.

Thankfully, the toilet was removed without any water damage. "Holler if you need me. Come on, Sheba." I raced up the stairs to the attic.

In the light of day, I couldn't miss the signs of someone having been there. Large footprints led from the window to the far side of the attic. A few boxes left behind were stacked in a corne; otherwise the large space was empty.

I opened the boxes first, knowing I wouldn't

find any treasure, but we'd need to clear them out to make room for our things. The first one held remnants of fabric someone might use to make a quilt. I'd donate them to the thrift store.

The second box, much larger than the first, held several colorful quilts. Why would someone leave them behind? I ran my hand over the top one, envisioning it on the bed. Absolutely gorgeous.

The third box held receipts from decades ago. It would be safe to throw them away.

Now, to search the room itself. I moved around the floor, testing each floorboard with my foot. None of them seemed loose. None seemed to have new nails. The footprints had led to the boxes I'd just opened, so I headed back there and ran my hands over the walls. Nothing.

Not yet admitting defeat, I moved to the bedroom across the hall. The sound of shattering tiles and rock music came from the master bath. Good. I hated the pink tile.

The same footprints were in the dust on the floor of the guest bedroom. This time, they led to a small walk-in closet. I reached up and pulled the cord over my head to turn on the light. Nothing had been left behind in here. I frowned. "Why leave behind the quilts and scraps of fabric?" I glanced at Sheba. "Other than a few pieces of ratty furniture, the previous owners had taken everything."

Her tail thumped the floor, stirring up dust.

"No luck?" Brad, his arms filled with a box of broken tile, poked his head into the room.

"Not yet. But, I know something is here."

"Okay. Good luck." He withdrew, his footsteps

fading. He seemed to be having the time of his life. Maybe demolition was therapy for some people. Unfortunately, I didn't want to go knocking down walls and pulling up floorboards.

"If I wanted to hide something of value in this house, Sheba, where would I put it?" I'd put it in the attic, but I'd checked there. The eaves. I dragged the ladder from outside and lugged it up the stairs to the attic.

"What are you doing? I'll get that." Brad took the ladder from me.

"I'm capable of climbing a ladder."

"You still won't be tall enough to reach the rafters in the attic without climbing to the very top."

"Fine. I want to see whether anything is stashed up there."

"Won't take but a minute." He flashed a grin and set up the ladder, scampering up it like a monkey. "Hey, there is something up here."

My heart thudded. "A bag of jewels?"

"No. The blueprints to the house. I was hoping to run across these somewhere." He dropped a tube down to me.

"There's nothing else?" My shoulders slumped.

"Nope." He climbed down. "I'm going to take a peek at these, then stop for lunch."

I nodded, starting to get hungry myself. "I'll fix the sandwiches." I'd stored the fixings in the fridge when we'd first arrived. The house wasn't yet to my liking, but it was livable. At least until the construction crew arrived tomorrow.

"You're going to like this." Brad waved for me to join him at the kitchen island.

"What?"

"This house has a hidden passage."

"Where?" I studied the blueprint which made absolutely no sense to me.

"Let's see if I can read this right." Holding the blueprint in front of him like a beacon, he stepped into the hall with me on his heels. "There should be a door in the wall under the stairs."

"There's a door under the stairs that looks like it could be used for storage."

"No, inside that."

"Why would someone put a hidden passage in this house?"

"Maybe whoever built it made moonshine."

Ah. I'd heard of people doing that during Prohibition. I reached out and opened the door, noting a lock that seemed broken, and stepped into the closet. The room was empty.

"Now, start pushing the panels on your left. One of them should open a door, I think."

I started tapping. The wall panels echoed back at me until I heard a soft click. To my right, a narrow door opened. "You're right!" I felt for a light switch. Not finding one, I reached overhead, found a dangling chain and pulled. Nothing. "We'll need a light. The bulb is burned out."

"Okay. Stay there. I'll be right back."

He returned a couple of minutes later with two flashlights. "Let me and the dogs go first. We don't know what condition this tunnel is in."

Nodding, I stepped back and turned on my light. When Brad ducked into the tunnel, I followed, keeping the light on the ground. A few roots had found their way through cracks in a brick wall, making watching where I put my feet imperative. "How far do you think it goes?" I asked.

"I'm going to guess it'll come out at one of the outbuildings." Brad shined his light forward. "This was definitely built a long time. Look." He pointed the light at a beam over our head.

Someone had carved the date of 1920 into the wood. Definitely a tunnel used by either those making moonshine or those transporting it. I loved owning a house with history.

Spring might have arrived to Waterfall, but underground, the dank air sent me shivering. I glanced overhead, trying to determine whether the house still stood above us or if we'd gone under the yard. The brick walls and dirt roof seemed secure. I didn't feel as if we'd be buried alive in minutes. Whoever had built the tunnel had been a master craftsman.

The tunnel sloped upward. To my right rose a set of steps made of large stones. To the front the tunnel continued.

"Let's see where door number one leads." Brad shoved his shoulder against the rotting wood. The door gave way in splinters. A few feet in, we stopped at a grate. Through the slats I could make out the inside of the storage shed.

"If every outbuilding has an entrance to the tunnel, then all the owners since 1920 knew about them. The outbuildings are definitely newer than the house." I glanced at Brad.

"The house was built by the father of the man I purchased it from. He did act rather pleased about me purchasing the place. I wonder whether we can find any information online about this place."

"I bet we can." I couldn't wait to open my laptop.

We continued down the tunnel to the end and climbed the last set of rock steps. The door there hung open, the lock broken. Brad held out a hand to stop me from going forward. "Wait. Something doesn't feel right."

"Be careful." The air coming from the other side smelled like something rotting.

Sheba whined and pressed close to my leg.

Barney barked.

Brad gagged and stumbled back. "There's a dead man." He put the back of his hand against his nose. "Been there a while."

"Where did the tunnel come out?"

"A cave of sorts. Not one of the outlying buildings."

"Do you know who the man is?"

He shook his head. "No. Let's head back and call McIlroy. I don't want to contaminate the crime scene in case it wasn't an accident."

It took less time rushing back to the house than it had going the other way. Death had a way of putting wings on our feet.

As soon as Brad stepped from the closet, he called McIlroy. "Found a decaying body about a football field's distance from the house. Uh huh. No idea. See you then." He hung up and met my gaze. "He'll be here in half an hour."

"What could you tell about the body?" I fell into a kitchen chair.

"Only that the man wore a suit." He sat across from me and folded his hands on top of the table. "Took some of the wind out of my sails. Until finding him, searching the tunnel had been fun."

"Yeah. A safe adventure for once, or so it seemed." I got up and retrieved my laptop. Maybe digging into the history of this house would divert me from the fact a man lay rotting on our property. I was deep into my research when McIlroy arrived.

"Local legend has it that the man who built this house made his money from robbing banks, but no one could ever prove it." I glanced up from reading as Brad went to answer the door. "Then, he moved on to making and selling moonshine. His son, the man you bought this house from, took over the family business, so to speak, by opening a bar. There's also a rumor he had a daughter who ran off at the age of seventeen. They never reconciled, leaving them with a son."

"You found all that?" He quirked a brow.

"Yep. There's a woman in Blytheville who has always been interested in local urban legends and writes up what she finds out. She added a disclaimer that it might not all be true, but it's what she's learned. We need to talk to this woman."

"Why?"

"Because she might know something about Queen."

Chapter Fourteen

McIlroy's eyes narrowed into slits. "Stay away from Queen. Don't make me tell you again."

"Don't you have a dead body to check on?" I arched a brow. "Besides, I'm not going to see Queen. Just whoever did the research on this house. I'm interested now that Brad and I own it." I looked to Brad for support.

"It would be nice to know more about this house, but don't go alone. Take someone with you and Sheba." He jerked his head toward the door. "I'll show you where the body is."

I sent Mom a quick text asking her to use her resources at the police station to find out how to contact the woman I wanted to see, then raced out the front door after the men. I reached Brad's rickety old truck that came with the house just as he closed his door and banged on the side of it. "I'll ride in the back, hold on," I yelled.

The detective tossed me a glare through the back window, but thankfully, Brad waited. I lowered the tailgate so Sheba and Barney could jump in, then climbed in after them. When I was ready, I banged on the window.

I should've taken into account that we'd be racing across a field. I bounced around the back of the truck like a beach ball. What was the hurry? The man was already dead. We hit one particularly deep hole, and I flew out, luckily landing on my feet, staring after the truck.

Great. I ran after them, ignoring the ache growing in my right ankle. By the time the truck stopped, I limped noticeably.

Brad climbed out of the truck, looked my way, and came running. "What happened?" He scooped me into his arms.

"I fell out when you drove over a big hole."

"Oh, sweetheart, I'm sorry. Are you hurt?" His chest rumbled.

"Are you laughing?" My mouth fell open as I glared at him.

"Not really."

"I could have been killed. I'm lucky all it did was hurt my ankle." I slapped his chest.

"Ow." His laughter increased as he sat me on the tailgate of the truck.

"Looks like she won't be getting into too much trouble now," McIlroy said.

"It's just a limp." I huffed and crossed my arms. "Glad to provide the two of you with entertainment."

"I'm sorry." Brad gave me a quick kiss. "I'll show McIlroy the body, then come tend to that ankle."

I nodded, hopping off the tailgate the second

they entered the cave. I didn't come all this way and get thrown out of a truck not to see what was going on. The smell slapped me harder inside the cave, and I pulled the neckline of my shirt over my nose.

"Do you know who it is?" Brad asked.

"Yep. Roy Clarkson. Son of the people who owned this house and property. They notified the police department last week that they haven't heard from their son in a while. Guess we know why. Someone shot the poor guy in the head."

I peeked around the men. "Why do you think he's wearing a suit out here?"

"My guess is he was meeting someone."

The someone who killed him. I shuddered and stepped outside while the detective called the crime scene techs.

Sheba was no longer in the back of the truck, so I limped in search of her. "Sheba? Here girl."

Something nefarious was going on at my new house, and I intended to find out what and put a stop to it. It all had to be tied to Jennings, Bill, and Ted. At least the three were involved or Jennings had been before he was killed.

I found Sheba and Barney digging at the base of a large oak tree. I dodged flying dirt to see what had my dog so enthralled she didn't come when I'd called her. "What did you two find?" Squeezing between them, I stared into a hole. The tip of a metal box peeked from the dirt the dogs hadn't dug up. Grabbing a nearby stick, I took over the excavation.

"What are you doing?" Brad spoke behind me. "You should be resting that ankle."

"The dogs found something." I gripped the breadbox-sized box and pulled it free. I couldn't pry the box open. "We'll never find the key."

"Let me try." Brad pulled his pocketknife from his jeans and pried the lid open. "Wow." He held it where I could see.

Rings, necklaces, and bracelets sparkled up at me like a pirate's treasure. "Looks like we found the stolen jewelry. I bet the other stolen items are around here somewhere. We need to search the cave."

"McIlroy said we can't go back in until the crime scene techs are finished."

"If anything is in there, they'll find it." I held up my hand for him to help me to my feet. My ankle had started to throb, and I was more than ready to ice and wrap it.

Leaning on Brad, I snapped my fingers for the dogs to follow and hobbled back to the truck. Brad hefted me onto the tailgate. "I'll be right back." He strode to the cave's entrance and called for the detective. Seconds later, he returned to me minus the box. "That's some find, Trin."

"I wonder how the dogs knew where to look."

"Freshly dug dirt, most likely. I'll take you back to the house. McIlroy said he'll catch a ride back with the techs."

"Should we leave him out here alone?" My eyes scanned the field. The cave that was little more than an overhang sat right where the thick woods began at the end of the property.

"He's armed and vigilant." Brad helped me into the front seat.

Back at the house, he wrapped my ankle with an ace bandage. "You brought a first aid kit?"

He glanced up from his ministrations. "Of course. I'm not an expert construction man. Accidents can happen. Like with you."

"I only fell out because you drove like Disney's Mr. Toad's Wild Ride."

"Again, I'm sorry." He patted my ankle and stood. "Do you want to go home? It's still early."

My phone vibrated. "I'm going to eat that sandwich I never had a chance to."

"Sit. I'll bring them."

I peered at my text. "It's from my mom. She said she can come pick me up. The lady who wrote the online article can talk to us now. Her name is May Lincoln."

"Okay. I'll meet you back home." He handed me my sandwich. "Promise me you'll be home by dark."

"I promise," I said between bites. "Since I'm in no condition to run anywhere, I'll play things very safe."

Brad wolfed down his sandwich and returned to the bathroom upstairs, leaving me to wait for my mother. She arrived within half an hour, her eyes narrowed at the bandage on my ankle. "What did you do?"

I filled her in on all that had happened that day while I went to grab my purse. "It's been exciting for sure."

"Sounds like it. Way more fun than my day. I had to bribe the girl to find me information on May Lincoln—expensive coffee for a week." She led the way to her car.

I let Sheba in the backseat and hobbled to the front passenger side. "If we get answers, it'll be worth it."

"You aren't the one spending five dollars a day." She started the car and drove toward town.

"I'm surprised she did anything on a Sunday."

"She works weekends. You can't shut down the police department like a nine-to-five job."

True. I shrugged. "Do you have any pain relief? My ankle is really bothering me."

"In my purse. I also brought an extra water bottle." She cut me a sideways look. "Are you sure you're up for this?"

"We'll be sitting, right? I'll be fine. Where are we meeting her?"

"At the diner. I thought a public place would be better than her home. What if she's mixed up in all this?" She pulled into the diner parking lot, half empty in the middle of the afternoon. "Look for a woman in a yellow dress."

"Stay, Sheba." I rolled the windows down, thankful the day was a mild one for spring. If I needed my fur baby, she'd jump out the window and come to my aid.

I limped after my mother, suddenly conscious of the clothes I wore. Jeans with holes in the knees and a tee-shirt stained with dirt from digging up the metal box. I sighed. Too late now. What an impression I'd make on Ms. Lincoln.

The hostess greeted us. "Two?"

"Oh, we're here to meet someone," Mom said. "There she is." She headed to a tiny, aged, woman in a yellow dress and hat. "Ms. Lincoln?"

"Yes. You must be Mrs. Ashford." Her eyes widened at me.

"Sorry. House renovations." I slid into the booth across from the woman, leaving the end for Mom. "My mother said you could give us some more information about the house my fiancé and I just bought."

"I know all about that house. My mother was a maid there back during Prohibition. She kept a journal." She slid a leather book across the table. "Did that once she figured out what was going on so if the police came, she could give them evidence that she didn't have anything to do with what the owners did."

"Your mother sounds very wise."

"I reckon she was." She leaned forward a bit. "Don't let that fall into the wrong hands, Missy. There are foul things afoot."

I dropped the book in my purse. "I promise to keep it safe and return it to you." I knew I'd be up late reading that night. "Have you eaten? Would you like to join us for lunch?"

"That won't be necessary, dear." She slid from the booth. "You keep that journal. After all, it's about your house." She smiled and strolled away with the good posture I wished I had.

"What a nice lady." I bumped Mom to let me out of the booth.

"I'd like to read that journal when you're finished."

"I'll tell you what it says."

"I know, but I'd still like to read it." She smiled.

"Journals written in the past have always fascinated me."

"Then, I'll be happy to lend it to you." I couldn't wait to dive between the pages. We'd find out something to help with this case for sure. "I'm thinking a visit to the assisted living home is our next step."

Mom glanced at her watch. "Wanna go now?"

"Tomorrow. You're off work, right? I can have Heather cover for me." I mentally checked my to-do list. "I don't want to leave Sheba in the car any more than I have to."

"Okay. I'll pick you up at nine. Come up with a reason for visiting the Clarksons, and how we can move the conversation to what's been going on. They know something, I guarantee it."

"I agree." I climbed into the car. "They may not be an active part of this crime ring right now, but I bet they once were and only stepped back because of their age. What I really want to know is who their daughter is." I removed the journal from my purse.

Most of what I wanted to know about her lay in these pages. I exhaled long and slow in an attempt to curb my excitement—like a child who'd been given a much-wanted Christmas gift.

"Okay, little Miss Clarkson. Who are you?"

Chapter Fifteen

Of course, Mom knew the receptionist at the assisted living home. She seemed to know just about everyone in town. Arriving there made me realize it had been too long since I'd visited my friends at the nursing home. Something I planned to remedy tomorrow. They'd be pleased to know Brad and I had set our wedding date.

"Sure, the Clarksons should be back in their apartment by now. Dinner was served an hour ago. Room 203." The receptionist smiled. "They don't have many visitors. Their son used to stop by once in a while but hasn't lately. Other than a woman, you two are the only ones."

"A woman?" My eyes widened at Mom. "Can you describe her?"

"Absolutely, although she never stops by the desk. Just waddles to the Clarkson's room. She's about your mother's height, middle-aged, frumpy, a bit hunched over."

Drat. Too old to be Queen. "Thank you."

We headed outside across a courtyard to what

could only be called a tiny house. Cute and efficient for an elderly couple that needed minimal help, but not enough to require a nursing home.

Mom knocked on the door of 203.

"Not today!" A man inside shouted. "You can't keep harassing us like this."

"Mr. Clarkson? It's Trinity Ashford. My fiancé, Brad Armstrong, bought your house. I'd like to ask you a few questions."

The door cracked open an inch. A dark eye studied us as if he didn't believe me. After several tense seconds, he opened the door. "I don't have a lot of time, so make it snappy. Gertie, we have company."

"Not Nellie again!"

"No, not her." He motioned to a sofa. "Sit. So, you bought the old place. How do you like it?"

"We're in the middle of renovations right now, but it's a lovely home." I held my purse containing the journal in my lap.

"Will be when you youngsters get finished." He reclined in his chair. "What do you want to know?"

"The history of the place?" I tilted my head. "We found blueprints that revealed a tunnel to the property border."

"My kin ran moonshine through that tunnel. Once, there was a gunfight between the family and federal agents. Lost a grandpa that day. Other than that, it's the same as any house." His eyes narrowed as his wife sat in a chair next to his. "Ain't that right, Gertie?"

"I love that house," she said. "Raised our children there, but now that they're on their own, it was too large for us to keep up."

They didn't know about their son yet. "How many children do you have?"

"Two. A boy and a girl." Her smile seemed forced, wavering a bit when she mentioned a daughter.

"How do you like it here?" Mom crossed her ankles, looking every bit as if we were making a friendly call to neighbors.

"Oh, we like it fine," she said. "Don't we, dear?"

"Yep. Lots of activities, and if we want, we can go to the dining hall for meals. Speaking of, it's getting late." He put his footrest down.

"We found an old doll in one of the bedrooms." I forced a laugh. "Rather creepy, actually. My fiancé and I like pulling pranks on each other with it. Do you want it back?"

"No way. Belonged to our daughter. She thought it mighty funny to hang it by its neck. Donate the thing." His eyes flashed. "That horrible deer painting we left, too."

The room one of the clowns had been in that night had belonged to their daughter. The plot thickened. "How can I contact your daughter? I'd like to see whether she wants the items back." No need to tell them both were locked up at the police station.

"You don't want anything to do with her."

"The receptionist mentioned she comes to visit you often," Mom said. "That's nice. My daughter and I are such good friends."

"She's no friend of ours." His face darkened.

"Why all the interest in her? You said you wanted to know about the house."

I stood, knowing we'd get nothing more from him. "I did. Thank you for your time. Come by and see the house sometime when we're finished."

Back in the car, I faced Mom. "If they're so estranged from their daughter, then why all the visits from her?"

"Remember how angry he was when we knocked? I think she's badgering them about something. Probably needs money." She turned the key in the ignition.

"Their son was shot in the head. What if she killed her brother?" I raised my brows. "Having grown up in that house, they'd have known about the tunnel. The clown had been in the room once occupied by the Clarkson daughter. He must have thought there was something still there."

"It almost sounds as if the brother might have been one of the clowns, but the time frame doesn't work."

I stared out the window as the sun set over the horizon. We learned little from Mr. and Mrs. Clarkson that we didn't already know. Hopefully, the journal would fill in some blanks.

Mom dropped me off in front of Brad's complex. I gave the doorman a distracted greeting and headed for the elevator.

Brad smiled up from the sofa. "How'd it go?"

"The old lady gave me a journal kept by her mother. I'm going to dig in before bed. Then, Mom and I paid a visit to the Clarksons. They really don't like their daughter." I sat next to him and cuddled close. "But, we didn't get a name. They also didn't seem to know about their son's death."

"It's strange that McIlroy hasn't notified them. That's usually done as soon as a body is identified." His arm curled around my shoulders.

What was happening with McIlroy's investigation? I could ask, but he'd tell me to keep my nose out of things and, if I didn't, he'd expect me to tell him everything I discovered. Definitely not a two-way street. I dug the journal out of my purse.

"Are you hungry?" Brad slipped away from me. "I picked up some ice cream on my way home."

"Now you're talking." I opened the journal and started reading.

Mrs. Lincoln's mother had been quite detailed in her daily writing. Some days held only a sentence or two, but many were pages long. She also wrote expansively on the fight between the Clarkson family and the feds. The woman also didn't pull back on her distaste for the devil's brew she called the moonshine. I smiled, wishing I could have met her and known the daughter better.

While the writing in the beginning was interesting, I needed to know more about the time before Brad purchased the house. I accepted the bowl of chocolate-chip ice cream, mumbled a thanks, and flipped through the pages until I almost fell asleep in my empty bowl.

Brad took the journal from my hands, closed it, then set it on the coffee table. "Come on. Time for bed." He took my hands and led me to the guest bedroom.

"Thanks." I'd read some more over breakfast and at work. As Brad headed to his room, I changed to my sleeping clothes, patted the bed for Sheba to join me, and fell asleep wondering why it was so hard to find out who the Clarksons' daughter was.

I woke the next morning before Brad and shuffled to the kitchen to make coffee. While it percolated, I opened the journal where I'd stopped the night before. A son was born, then two years later, a girl. Nellie Mae Clarkson. The pages described two spoiled children used to getting their own way by sassing their parents. After discovering the tunnel, they hid for such a long time their parents had called the police. My parents would've spanked me way before I could do anything to frighten them that way.

"Good morning." Brad entered the kitchen and poured two cups of coffee, handing me one. "Are you still going to want your frou-frou coffee?"

"Does the sun rise every morning?" I lifted my face for a kiss. "This cup is an appetizer."

"Finding anything interesting in those pages?" He sat across from me, already dressed in a suit for work.

"The kids were brats, but their parents seemed to love them anyway." I closed the journal and slipped it into my purse. "I'd better get ready for work."

I raced to the room and fumbled through a drawer for clean clothes. "Need to do laundry."

"I'll call someone up."

Sometimes wealth made life so easy. I found a clean pair of knit pants and a flowered tunic, put my hair into a ponytail, and rushed back to the kitchen to finish my coffee. Why was it that coffee didn't taste good when it cooled down, but a frozen, blended coffee was delicious?

I tossed the rest down the sink. "I'm ready. Actually, I'm going to drive myself because I want to pay a visit to the nursing home after work."

"Sounds good. I'll be working late anyway. There's another vacant strip mall I'm considering."

We went to the parking garage together, then went our separate ways. Not far, actually, since only a large parking lot separated the doggy day care from the theater. A beep of my horn, then I turned behind my store to park.

"Another day of work, girl." I unlocked the back door and let Sheba in ahead of me, a habit I'd started a few months back. This way, if someone lay in wait, I'd have plenty of warning.

No one jumped out at us. I locked the back door and stored my purse behind the counter. What I wanted to do was read more of the journal. What I needed to do was check emails, reservations, and whatever else the day presented. What I did do was prop my chin in my hands and stare out the window.

The answer to this case was right in front of my face. Sitting there on the counter, but I was still oddly reluctant to open the journal. What would I do with the information I found? Give it to McIlroy or go in search of the daughter myself or both?

"Why so maudlin?" Shar asked, coming in through the front door. "You look miles away."

I told her what Mom and I had done the night

before, tapping the journal. "Why hasn't McIlroy told the Clarksons their son is dead?"

"I've wondered the same thing myself." She locked her purse behind the counter. "He's been very hush-hush over this whole murder case. I think the person behind it all is someone the department doesn't want to mess with."

"Hm." I opened the journal and started to read. So engrossed was I in the story of my house I barely noticed when Brad brought my coffee treat.

He laughed. "You'll not get a thing out of her until she's done." He kissed the top of my head and left.

"That man knows you so well," Shar said.

"Shh. The daughter's about to leave the house after a huge blowup with her father."

"How old is she? Is there a description of her?" Shar leaned over the counter.

"Sixteen. Yes. Dark hair, blue eyes, and an attitude that the world owes her." A lot like most teenagers.

"What did they fight about?"

"The daughter wanted to branch off of the family business. Seems she didn't want to manage a string of bars and nightclubs. She wanted to make money by having others do the dirty work. Her father told her that wasn't the way the family operated." I straightened and sipped my drink, my mind whirling.

Shar chewed the inside of her lip. "Who do we know that Alex is hesitant to deal with" and lets others do her dirty work?"

"Queen." I shuddered.

Chapter Sixteen

Now what? I had no desire to see the woman but knew there was a day in the near future when we'd come face-to-face again.

"This is bad." Shar paced in front of the counter. "This is really, really bad. Once she knows we know, she'll send someone for us. They won't be friendly."

"Maybe she won't find out. I mean, Brad and I have been renovating the house and not found anything of value inside. Since nothing has been printed in the paper about the jewels we found in the woods, she might not suspect us of anything."

Shar whirled to face me. "We need something to give her if she comes."

I nodded. "The identity of whoever double-crossed her." That seemed like an impossible task, but I suspected Bill or Ted. "I have a sudden need of a plumber."

"What are you going to do? Just ask them outright?"

"I'm not sure exactly, but I want them to think

we know it's them and will go to Queen unless they give us part of the loot." It would be risky, but the two men didn't seem that bright. Not if they were going against Queen.

I sucked harder on my straw. There were holes in my plan. Big ones. I only hoped I didn't fall into one of them. "I need to keep thinking on it because I'm pretty much winging things at this point." Grabbing my phone, I called the plumbing company about a clogged drain. No turning back now. "Queen didn't seem that interested in Bill and Ted, though."

"I have a feeling they aren't the ones doing the double cross." Shar crossed her arms. "It has to be someone close to her, but we have no idea who that would be."

"Maybe we'll find out this afternoon when the plumbers arrive. Either way, we're stirring the pot."

"Alex is going to blow a gasket." Shar shook her head. "We need to at least let him know Queen's real name."

"You're right." I sent him a quick text about the journal and coming to the conclusion the Clarksons' daughter was Queen. I also let him know she'd been paying them regular visits disguised as a frumpy woman.

He replied almost immediately with all caps. "STOP SNOOPING!"

I showed Shar the text. She nodded. "Yep. A gasket. I'm surprised he hasn't locked me up for my own protection."

"He's threatened to." I glanced at Sheba, reassured that no one would harm me while she was around. I snapped my fingers. "Didn't it strike you as odd that Queen found out so much about Bill and Ted in one hour? That's because she already had the information. Which confirms to me that they do work for her."

"Why the pretense?"

"She's playing games with us." The question was why? I'd never met the Clarksons before. Brad purchased the house, and that was the first time he'd met them. Why would a loan shark be interested in toying with me? Unless, she'd known about Brad purchasing the property. Could she have been interested in the place herself and wanted to run us out with a dangerous game? I felt pretty certain I'd hit the nail on the head. That underground tunnel would be priceless to a crook. "I think Queen is trying to drive me and Brad out of our house."

"Makes sense to me. Plumber coming."

Drat. Only one of them strolled toward the store. Maybe just one would be more willing to talk.

I glanced at Shar. "We'll talk about meeting Queen at the casino and see what happens." I smiled as the plumber entered. "The drain is in the grooming station on the other side of this glass." His nametag read Bill.

"Okay." He headed for the back, casting several glances on the way.

I motioned for Shar to follow me to where the man could hear us talking. "You ready for another visit to the casino?"

"Sure am. Need to pay a visit to Queen. Don't want anyone hitting me over the kneecaps."

I rolled my eyes and mouthed for her to

downplay the meeting. "She didn't seem that bad."

"Change of subject." She mouthed that Bill was staring our way. "How are the renovations coming?"

"Good. Workers have been out there this week." I forced what I hoped was a normal laugh. "With a house that old, I'd hoped to find treasure buried in the walls. So far, nothing."

"There's nothing wrong with this drain, ma'am." Bill moved toward us, his sharp eyes darting from me to Shar and back to me.

"Really?" I widened my eyes. "I honestly thought it backed up this morning."

"Nope. Have a good day." He strode out of the store. Once he stepped off the sidewalk, he whipped around and faced the shop window. Our eyes clashed through the window.

"Now, we wait." I smiled, certain I'd be hearing from Queen by the end of the day.

"When you decide to get involved in sleuthing, you bring the danger." Shar shook her head. "I have a grooming appointment outside of town. See you later."

"Stay safe." I settled behind my desk, wishing it wasn't Heather's day off. Now that I'd stirred the proverbial pot, I didn't want to be alone.

I quickly read the rest of the journal. While interesting, it told me nothing new. I slid it into my desk drawer to lend to Mom whenever she stopped by.

Brad texted me to see whether I wanted to go out to lunch. When I told him I was at the store alone, he said he'd bring something over. Good. I wanted to fill him in on what I'd discovered.

He brought two chef salads from a local restaurant, and we sat at the table near the window. "How's your day?"

"A little slow businesswise," I said. "But picking up speed on Jennings' death. Well, actually I don't have a suspect for his death, but—" I told him of my suspicions about Queen.

Brad grew quiet for a bit before speaking. "No wonder Mr. and Mrs. Clarkson were in such a hurry to sell. They must have known their daughter wanted the house. Unfortunately, their decision has put us in danger."

"Do you think she would've still come if I wasn't investigating?"

He nodded. "When she sent the clowns, she didn't expect anyone to be in the house." With his fork, he moved the salad around on his plate. "McIlroy notified the Clarksons about their son's murder this morning. They accused the daughter."

"They're probably right."

"He suggested they go into witness protection, but they've refused."

"What will happen to their businesses?"

He shrugged. "Sold, I guess. I'm not interested in bars and nightclubs. Once Queen is convicted—if she ever is—the businesses will be left to the son."

She'd be behind bars if I had anything to say. I had a knack for persuading people to either say too much and incriminate themselves or try to kill me. Either way they were locked up.

After work, I stayed true to my commitment to visit my friends at the nursing home. Margie, Hank, and Frank waved me to their table.

"Let me grab a plate first." I headed to the buffet and loaded my plate with fried chicken, green beans, and mashed potatoes with gravy. Then, I joined my friends. "Sorry, it's been a while since I've visited."

"That's all right, sweetie." Margie patted my hand. "We know you're busy. I bet you're neck deep in trouble again, aren't you?"

"That I am. But, I do have good news." I smiled. "Brad and I are getting married at the lake on June fifth."

"It's about time." Frank clapped his hand on the table. "Life is too short to put things off."

"That is good news," Hank said, "but I want to hear about the trouble."

I told them everything. "Do any of you know the Clarksons?"

"Sure, we do." Margie sighed and shook her head. "Those kids caused a lot of problems as teenagers. It's not a surprise that they've grown into scoundrels."

"Any idea where Nellie lives?"

"No, but you can bet it will be in an upscale neighborhood. Only expensive things for her."

So, she would've only wanted the house for the tunnel. Not to live in unless she planned on fixing it up like Brad and I were. Too bad. I'd fallen in love with the place and wanted my little farm.

"The parents are frightened of her." I took a bite from my chicken.

"Of course, they are." Margie clicked her tongue. "I remember a time she screamed in her mother's face because she wouldn't buy her an expensive pair of boots. When the kids were growing up, the family had money, but as you know, running a business also costs money."

I nodded. Hopefully, McIlroy had put a guard on Queen's parents. The tighter the noose around her neck, the harder she'd fight. I intended to make sure it tightened real fast.

After supper, I returned to my car and frowned. Someone had put a flier on the windshield. I shook my head and removed it. A person couldn't even go to a nursing home without someone trying to sell her something. I slid into the driver's seat and glanced at the flier. Not an advertisement at all.

"What do you think you're doing?" Signed with a big curly Q.

143

Chapter Seventeen

Crumpling the note, I threw it on the floor. I knew exactly what I was doing, and that was setting out to catch a killer. I called Shar and asked if she was up to a stakeout.

"It's like you don't even know me, Trinity. Of course, I am. I'll call your mother. How are we going to get away from the men?"

"We're going out for coffee. Meet me at the diner as soon as you can." Not a lie, exactly. We would stop for coffee before heading to the high-falutin' neighborhood Queen might live in. I hung up and texted Brad that I was going out for coffee.

Brad called immediately. "You're up to something."

"What makes you say that?"

"I know you. What are you going to do?"

"Margie told me that Queen might live in that fancy neighborhood in Scanton. Shar, Mom, and I are going to see if we can discover where she lives." I filled him in on the rest of my visit with them. "I don't plan on getting out of the car. If I do find out where she lives, I'll let McIlroy know."

"Since he hasn't discovered the address, she must have purchased under an alias."

"Yep. Oh, and there was a note on my car." I recited it to him.

"That almost sounds like a warning?"

"*Almost* being the magic word. I'll keep my phone on so you'll know where I am every second."

"Be careful. I'll wait up. Love you."

"I love you." I smiled, started the car, and drove to our local, and only, coffee shop.

"Long night ahead?" The barista asked. "I don't think I've ever seen you in here this late."

"Girls' night out. I'll need a pick-me-up." I paid for my drink and settled in at a table to wait for Mom and Shar.

"'What do you think you're doing' could mean anything, right? It didn't sound exactly like a threat. I sipped my drink. If it was from Queen, how did she know I was at the nursing home? Was I being followed? With a frown, I peered out the window.

Cars lined the street. I made note of everyone I could see, then studied the customers in the shop. A man reading a newspaper in the corner. Another on his laptop. Two women at a table close to mine chatted about an upcoming sale at a department store. Another man in a hoodie slouched in a chair, headphones on. None of them seemed interested in me in the slightest.

I stood and stepped outside the door, checking to see if anyone sat in the car within sight of the coffee shop. With the sun setting, it was hard to tell. I waved as Mom and Shar drove by in search of a parking spot, then returned to my table.

Five minutes later, Mom and Shar rushed in, ordered their coffees, and the three of us headed for my car. Shar frowned. "Why your car?"

"Because you brought the Thunderbird, and it sticks out too much." I opened the door. "We're stopping by my place quick to get Sheba. She's the best warning signal we can have."

"Anyone have trouble getting away from their man?" Mom asked. "I simply told Joe what we were doing. He said to be careful. Easy."

"He was watching TV, wasn't he?" I glanced at her in the rearview mirror.

"Not my fault he wasn't paying attention." She laughed.

"Alex wasn't home from work yet, so I left him a note that I would be hanging with the two of you for a while. No lies but no outright explanation either." Shar grinned.

"I was completely upfront with Brad." After he called me, but they didn't need to know that bit of information. "Help me keep an eye out behind us." I told them of the note. "I want to know whether I'm being followed, because there's no way Queen or any of her goons could've known I visited the nursing home unless they followed me."

Mom turned in the seat. "Any idea what kind of a car we're looking for?"

I described the ones I'd seen in front of the coffee shop. "I know it's a long stretch, but—"

"Makes sense to me." Shar kept her gaze on the side mirror.

I parked in front of Tail Waggin' and left the car

running while I went upstairs to get Sheba. Always eager to go with me, she bounded outside, did her business, then jumped into the backseat when Mom opened the door.

"Let's get this show on the road." Shar rubbed her hands together. "We have a twenty-minute drive."

"Yes, ma'am." I turned the car around and sped from the parking lot. Hopefully, the police were lying low because I intended to push the limit. The stakeout might have been my idea, but I did work in the morning and had no idea how big this swanky neighborhood was.

"This is going to be a longshot, you know." Shar bent over and picked up the note I'd thrown on the floor. She unfolded it, read it, then glanced at me. "You didn't tell us you'd received a threat."

"I'm not sure that's what it is."

"It has to be from Queen. Who else?"

I shrugged. "I agree it's probably from her. That's why I said I'm being followed. It was on my car after visiting the nursing home."

"Maybe I should have made sure your father knew what we were doing and where we were going," Mom said.

"Why? I told Brad, and he can track us on my phone."

"Because I'm pretty sure that car behind the truck behind us is following us."

"Oldest trick in the book." Shar dropped the paper. "Keeping one car between you and your prey."

I peered in the rearview mirror. "Keep an eye on

it. I'm going to take the next exit." I whipped in front of another vehicle and veered onto the exit. The truck behind me went on, but the car stayed behind us.

I took a quick left, then another right, circling back to the freeway. The car continued to follow. "We can't head to Scanton until we lose them."

"Turn right up here. There's a police station half a mile up. That'll convince them to leave us alone."

Worth a try. I followed her instructions and parked in front of a station, smaller than the one we had in Waterfall. The car following us blocked the entrance to the lot.

"We're sitting targets," Mom whispered. "Are they going to kill us right here? That would be embarrassing."

"Why are you whispering and why embarrassing?" I turned and stared out the back window wondering whether I should honk until an officer came out.

"Killed in front of the police department?" Her voice rose. "What are we going to do?"

"Let's see if they do anything. I can always honk if things become dicey." I backed up and turned the car around to face the other vehicle. No reason to show any sign of weakness. I turned my brights on.

"You're antagonizing them." Mom slapped me on the shoulder.

"Trying to figure out what they plan to do." Eventually they'd tire of the showdown, right?

My phone rang.

We all shrieked.

"It's Brad. Hello?"

"Why are you stopped at the police station in Burrows?"

"Uh, a car was following us, and this was the closest safe place. We should be able to leave soon."

"That was a very bad idea. Stay safe." Brad told me he loved me and hung up. He'd sounded as if he was trying not to sound angry.

My poor man. I did put him through turmoil, yet he still wanted to marry me. Which reminded me I needed to hurry and take Mom's wedding dress to be altered.

"I hate this sitting around," Shar huffed. "Maybe we should go to them. What if they only want to talk? If they wanted to kill us, all they had to do was start shooting." She pulled her gun from her purse. "Want me to start the shootout?"

"Are you nuts?" I pushed her hand down. "That would be one way to alert the police inside and get arrested."

Sheba stuck her massive head between me and Shar, her gaze on the other car. Her ears stood at attention.

Both front doors of the other vehicle opened.

Chapter Eighteen

I laid on the horn.

The doors on the other car slammed shut, and the car burned rubber out of the parking lot.

"We'd better get out of here before the police come." Shar clicked on her seatbelt. "Go in the opposite direction of that car."

Not wanting to be detained for questioning, I followed Shar's advice. We entered Scanton far later than I'd wanted. Ten o'clock was bedtime.

"So, which house is hers?" Mom, having unhooked her seatbelt, leaned her arms on the front seats.

"Fiddlesticks. I have no idea." I parked in front of a wrought-iron gate. "Plus, these homes are all fenced. We have no choice but to walk."

"We're going to get caught." Shar shoved her door open. "You didn't think this through very well."

No, I didn't. I slid out and clipped Sheba's leash to her collar. "We're simply three women out walking our dog at ten o'clock at night."

"Right," Mom said. "Not suspicious at all."

We didn't know what kind of car Queen drove, whether she lived in a ranch-style house or a two-story, or even on which street. I definitely hadn't done enough research. It wasn't likely she'd simply drive down the street. Although, we'd been lucky before.

I figured since she worked out of the casino she kept late hours. But, it had been in the middle of the day when we ate lunch with her. So, yeah, we knew virtually nothing. I exhaled heavily.

"Don't look, but I think the car that followed us earlier is cruising down the street," Shar said.

Mom and I turned. It did look like the same car.

"I said, don't look! We need to hide."

"This hedge will do." I pulled Sheba behind a well-manicured hedge and peered around it as the car cruised slowly past. I couldn't tell if the driver was a man or a woman. "I think we should try to follow that car."

"Going to be hard to do with all these streetlights. The place is lit up like a prison." Shar stood and peered over the hedge. "It's passed."

"Since the driver didn't see anything, hopefully they won't look in the rearview mirror." I clutched Sheba's leash. "If it is the same vehicle, they're looking for us. If they saw my car, they know we're here. Maybe they'll lead us to Queen." A lot of ifs, but they actually made sense. At least to me.

The car turned left at the end of the street causing us to jog in order not to lose sight of it. As we rounded the corner, the taillights turned left again. With such large lots, the corners were far apart and it wasn't long before my chest heaved.

"Running is not my favorite thing." Mom stopped and bent over, her hands on her knees.

"Mine either. Stay here, and I'll try to keep the car in sight." With Sheba happily running alongside me, we continued to follow the vehicle.

Just when I thought I might have an actual heart attack, the car stopped and entered a gate that swung open. Gasping for breath, I peered through the bars of the fence at a salmon-colored mansion. I'd bet my favorite pair of boots we'd found Queen's house.

I stepped back and studied the six-foot fence with ornate spikes along the top. I could scale it if someone gave me a boost, but I'd tear something in the process. Still, I couldn't see another way in but over the top.

Red and blue lights flashed behind me.

I whirled, startled as an officer slid out of a squad car. His tag identified him as Johnson. "Uh, hello?"

"Trying to find a way in?" He crossed his arms, a frown on his face.

"No, uh, just admiring the house." Oh, pooh. It sounded false even to my ears.

"Name."

I sighed. "Trinity Ashford."

"Where are your friends?"

"Huh?"

"We received a call about three women and a big dog roaming the streets. Now, here you are trying to figure out how to scale that fence." His frown deepened as Mom and Shar raced to my side.

"We're perfectly legit, officer." Shar smiled. "I'm engaged to Detective McIlroy of Waterfall PD."

"If that's true, I'm sure he wouldn't be happy to see the three of you out here."

"Actually, he wouldn't be surprised in the slightest." She put her hands on her hips.

"In the car, ladies. The dog, too."

I scrambled for the door. If we stayed outside attracting attention, Queen would know we'd found her house. We could sort everything out at the station. "Will my car be okay?"

"This is a nice neighborhood, Miss Ashford. At least until you three came along." Once we squeezed into the back, he climbed in the front and drove to the station.

"Alex is going to kill me," Shar whispered. "He'll never buy the story we were sightseeing at this time of the night."

"Shh." I jerked my head toward the officer. "I think we found Queen's house." I met the officer's gaze in the rearview mirror.

His eyes narrowed, but he didn't say anything. Perhaps he'd heard of me. That could or could not work in our favor.

"We'll talk later," I whispered.

At the station, Officer Johnson put us in a holding cell with two skimpily dressed women. At least he didn't cuff us.

"What did they get you three for?" One of them asked, her gaze on Sheba.

"Walking our dog too late at night in a ritzy neighborhood we don't live in," Shar said. "You?"

"Soliciting." She grinned. "We're here on a regular basis. It's no big thing. I spend at least one night a month here. I'm Ginger. That's Lacey."

"Sometimes more," the other said with a laugh. "I feel like I should give Officer Johnson a Christmas card every year."

"Are you sure it's Queen's house?" Mom asked.

"Not a hundred percent, but that's where the car following us went. I didn't see an easy way in."

"You can't possibly be crazy enough to mess with that woman." Ginger's eyes widened. "She'd kill you as soon as look at you."

"What can you tell us about her?" I leaned forward.

"Why do you want to know? Ow." She glared at Lacey who'd elbowed her.

"She's threatening me."

"Then, I'd run rather than confront her," Lacey said. "We don't want to talk about her."

"Please. I can't keep my family safe unless I know all I can." I gave her an imploring look.

"She has her fingers into every sort of crime around these parts." Ginger shook her head. "She ain't our john, but she's got girls. Mostly, she lends money and breaks kneecaps."

"Is she into jewels and fine art?"

"You betcha." She leaned against the block wall behind the bench she sat on. "I've never been in her house, but I've heard she has a whole gallery full of stolen paintings. No one goes in there but her. I've heard there's a secret door to get in."

Made sense because of the tunnel in my house. I leaned against the wall behind me. Queen was a busy woman, but that didn't tell me how to draw her out. Obviously, she didn't want me dead or I would be. So, what were her plans regarding me? For the first time since getting involved in mysteries, I longed for another note on my windshield.

Sensing McIlroy would most likely make us spend the night, I scooted to the floor and lay down, using Sheba for a pillow. I woke to sunlight streaming through the thin window and McIlroy scowling through the bars of our cell. "I hope you let Brad and my father know where we were."

"I did." He motioned for Officer Johnson to open the cell. "Neither of them are pleased."

"Are we going to be arrested?" Shar asked, for once not flirting with her man.

"No, but you should be." He didn't smile, only turned to lead us from the station. "I'll take you to your car, Trinity. Shar, you'll go home with me." He shook his head. "I've warned you of the dangers involved with Queen. Now, I hear you were outside her house. Do you three have a death wish?"

"No." I crossed my arms. "But I do want to know what she wants from me."

"You might not learn that this side of the grave." His face darkened. "Climb in the car."

You could have cut the silence with a chainsaw on the ride back to my vehicle. Even Sheba's ears drooped. I dreaded the lecture I'd receive when at home. "Brad knew what we were doing," I mumbled.

"Then he's as foolish as the three of you." McIlroy sent me a sharp glance in the rearview mirror.

"I prefer to call it supportive." Mom pursed her lips. "We're grown women, Detective. You can't treat us like children. Short of locking us up, you can't do anything."

He laughed and instead of taking us to my car, took us to the police station in Waterfall and locked us up, except for Sheba. "Your dog doesn't deserve this. We'll collect your car, Miss Ashford. Ladies." He spun and marched away.

What just happened? Mouth open, I stared at Mom and Shar. "Way to dare him, Mom."

She plopped on the stainless-steel bench. "Just sit. We might be here for a few hours."

"I have a business to run." I dialed Heather and explained I would be detained and was unable to open the store.

"No worries. I'll take care of everything. I hope you're okay?"

"Just busy." I definitely didn't want to spread the word I was behind bars. The gossip mill would never end.

"Cell phones." Officer Snowe held her hand between the bars.

I huffed and handed it over. "You can't keep us here without arresting us."

"We can for a bit." She gave a thin-lipped smile. "It's about time you three learned a lesson."

I curled my lip and took my seat. Thankfully, I rarely had to speak with Officer Snowe, but when I did, I didn't like the experience.

Hours passed with no sign of McIlroy, the other officers, or our significant others. I wanted to bang my head on the wall. Instead, I thought about Queen and how I could find out what she wanted. Did she think I had something? I'd found the doll, the painting, and the jewels. Did she think I still had the jewels? Did she even know I'd found them?

Again, I had more questions than answers.

"How long can they hold us?" Mom asked.

"Seventy-two hours. Might as well relax." Shar shrugged. "Alex can be very stubborn."

"I can't be here for three days. I have a business to run."

"And who is going to answer the phones here? They might fire me." Tears welled in her eyes.

"He's only trying to teach us a lesson." Shar crossed her arms. "I can be just as stubborn. I hope the food is good in this joint."

I knew Brad would care for my pets, but I couldn't have Heather responsible for the shop. She had a family. I moved to the bars and called for the detective.

"What?"

"What do we have to do to get out of here?" I gripped the bars hard enough to make my knuckles hurt.

"Promise not to go looking for Queen." His eyes flashed.

"That's it?" I couldn't promise not to go looking for her, but I couldn't say she wouldn't come looking for me. "Fine. I promise." I smiled.

"I don't believe you."

"Pinky swear. I will not go looking for Queen." I'd already found her house. All I needed to do was convince her to come out and play.

CYNTHIA HICKEY

Chapter Nineteen

The phone rang the next morning before I could unlock the front door. Thinking it must be an emergency since it wasn't eight o'clock yet, I rushed to answer. "Tail Waggin' Pet Daycare. This is Trinity, how may I help you?"

The person on the other end sighed before speaking. "I must admit I'm a bit surprised that you would come snooping around my house."

I sat in my chair and propped my feet on the shelf under the counter. "I wanted to ring your doorbell and ask you what you want with me."

"There are just two things I want from you. The first being the doll that once hung in my bedroom. The second is that painting."

"I don't have them. The police took them when the doll showed up unexpectedly at my house."

She stayed silent for a moment. "What do you mean?"

"I mean that creepy old thing showed up at my apartment. I thought my fiancé put it there as a joke and reciprocated. Turns out that neither of us

159

removed it from the house. Now, the police have both of those items." I drummed my fingers on the desk. "I'm thinking you might have an employee who isn't completely trustworthy. Are you aware your brother was murdered?"

"No." Her voice lost its superior tone. "Tell me."

"I'm sure you're aware of the tunnel under the house?"

"Yes."

I told her of Brad and me following it and finding her brother dead. I left out the fact the dogs had dug up a box of jewels. Not feeling as if I could trust her quite yet, I continued. "When my friends and I were on our way to your place last night, a car with two people inside followed us. That same car turned into your drive and entered through the gate. Mind telling me who they are and why they were following me?"

She laughed. "That would be Bill and Ted. I told them to shadow you and take those two items if they made contact. Unfortunately, you're a bit smarter than they are."

"Who would double-cross you?"

"Darling, it could be a number of people."

"But why include me?"

"Obviously, like me, they think you have something they want."

"What's in the doll, Nellie?" I put a finger to my lips as Brad entered the store with the day's coffee.

"Ah. You know who I am. I'm guessing you've visited my parents."

"I have. They don't seem to like you much."

"No, my brother was their favorite. You bring me those two items, and I'll show you why I want them. I'll call you tomorrow to see whether you were successful." Click.

Brad set the coffees on the table by the window and waited for me to join him. "Why is Queen calling you?"

"She wants the doll and the painting." I had no idea how to get them away from McIlroy.

"Can we trust her?" His brow furrowed as he sipped his drink.

"To a point, I think." I twirled my cup on the table. I should call McIlroy. I'd promised not to go looking for Queen, and I didn't. Would he consider her calling me breaking that promise? "I have to call the police station."

"Want me to?"

"Sure. McIlroy isn't mad at you." I sure wished I knew who Queen's employees were. If I did, I could be working down the list to find out who was trying to make it appear as if Queen was after me. Who was double-crossing her?

"Better yet," he said as Heather entered the store, "we should go to the station and speak to him in person."

I made a face, not wanting to step foot in that building for a long time. "Fine. We won't be gone long, Heather." I patted Sheba's head, telling her she wasn't going with me this time.

"No worries." Heather put her purse away. "I'll take care of the boarding animals, then unpack the boxes that came in yesterday."

"You're a peach." I grabbed my bag and

followed Brad to his Mercedes. "How are you going to persuade him to give us those items?"

My phone rang. "Mom's calling." I put the phone to my ear. "Hey."

"Don't you have a dress-fitting today?"

Oops. I'd forgotten. "At five-thirty. Come to the shop when you leave work."

"Okay. I have the dress in my car."

"See you in a few." I glanced at Brad. "Almost forgot about my dress-fitting. How are things going on your end?"

"Good. Caterer is set up, reception booked for the country club, and tuxes just came in." He grinned. "I had no idea a wedding could be put together this fast."

"The key is determination." I sipped my drink as he drove.

"As to getting the items," Brad continued, "the authorities have been after Queen for a long time. If McIlroy thinks giving us back the doll and painting will draw her out, he'll hand them over easy enough."

True. The trick would be Queen taking them from us without getting caught. I had no idea how she would accomplish such a task.

Mom glanced up from the reception desk when we entered the police station. "I didn't think 'see you in a few' was meant literally."

"We'd like to speak to McIlroy." I leaned on the desk.

"I'll let him know. Have a seat." She reached for her phone.

Three hard plastic chairs sat against the wall. A

snoring drunk sat in one, leaving the other two for us. Even with Brad taking the middle seat, the alcoholic fumes from the other man almost gagged me. I pulled the neckline of my tee-shirt over my nose.

When McIlroy motioned us to follow him, I couldn't go fast enough. He led us to a small conference room and told us to have a seat. From the stern look on his face, I guessed he thought we were there about more threats to my life.

"What is it this time?" He folded his hands on the tabletop.

"Queen called me this morning. I don't know how she found my number." I mimicked his posture.

"She has a lot of resources. What does she want?"

"The doll and the painting."

His brows shot to his hairline. "Did she say why?"

"No, but said she'd show me once she had them. I also think, and she agrees, that someone who works for her is double-crossing her. She admitted to having Bill and Ted follow me so they could ask for those things. Except, I never let them get close enough." I relaxed against the back of the chair. "If you give us those things, I'll lead you right to her."

"She's smarter than that, or she would've been caught by now."

"Why hasn't she? Surely, you knew she operated out of the casino."

"Every time we sent someone to apprehend her, someone warned her and she disappeared. We didn't know Nellie Clarkson was also Queen. Had no reason to suspect her under her real name." He shook his head. "The department really let this one slide under the radar. She's a very dangerous and smart woman. I'm not sure about you meeting with her."

"If she's as bad as you say, then I'd be dead by now."

"Not if she thought you had what she wanted. Now, she knows you don't."

I leaned my elbows on the table and stared into his eyes. "I don't think she wants to harm me. She's actually impressed by me. Thinks my crime-solving is interesting."

He glanced at Brad. "What do you think?"

"Put a tracker on the doll and let Trinity meet with her in a safe place. That way, Trinity can be gone when you arrest the woman, but you'll know where she is at all times." He smiled at me. "I don't want Trin in danger if there's shooting."

McIlroy rubbed his hands briskly over his face, the stress of this investigation showing in his slumped shoulders and bloodshot eyes. "You're right. It's a risk, but we need to stop that woman. Wait here."

"If I would've suggested that, he wouldn't have agreed." I frowned.

"I don't annoy him quite as much as you do." Brad gave me a one-armed hug. "Don't fret. Just be happy he's giving them to us."

McIlroy returned with the doll and the painting. "We've gone over both of these thoroughly and not found anything worthwhile."

"Maybe they're sentimental." I turned the doll over so it wasn't staring at me.

"Sign this." McIlroy handed us a sheet of paper and an ink pen. "I have to note who I released the items to."

I scribbled my signature. "Thanks." I stood and gathered Queen's things, more than happy to return them to their owner. No way did I want either one to end up back at my house.

The rest of the day was normal, at least as normal as my life was when not involved in a murder investigation. Poor Mr. Jennings, thief or not, still didn't have justice for his death. This might be a time when the killer remains unidentified and gets away.

"I want to go with you when you meet with Queen," Shar said, as I locked up for the day. "You shouldn't go alone."

"Fine with me as long as she doesn't specify that I come alone. See you tomorrow." I practically skipped to my car. I was finally having Mom's wedding dress tailored to fit me. The shop also had some veils for me to choose from.

Mom drove up, honked her horn, then rolled down the window. "Want me to follow you or the other way around?"

"You can lead." We'd decided to drive separately so we wouldn't have to come back to the store.

I followed her to the shop in the center of town and waited while she removed the dress from her trunk. "Let me carry it in, please." The wedding grew more real with each day.

"You must be Trinity Ashford. I'm Ann." A stylish woman greeted us. "We've champagne in the viewing area. Let me take the dress for you. Follow me, please."

While Mom sat and sipped from a flute, I followed Ann to a dressing room. She hung the dress on a hook. "I'll be right here when you're ready."

I quickly pulled off my clothes and slipped into Mom's satin gown. I didn't quite fill in the bodice, and the hem dragged more than it should, but I knew once tailored, I'd feel like a princess. "I'm ready." I skimmed my hands over my hips, liking the softness.

Ann clipped the dress in certain spots, making the dress magically fit like a second skin. Wow. I couldn't believe how gorgeous and sexy a dress from the 1950s could look. Brad's eyes were going to pop out of his head.

Mom started crying when I strolled into view. "Oh, my."

"I feel the same." Tears pricked my eyes as I climbed on the raised platform to view myself from every angle. "Ann, you're wonderful."

"It's a beautifully elegant dress." She clasped her hands in front of her. "The groom is a lucky man."

No, I was the lucky one. I stared at myself for a few more minutes, then carefully stepped off the platform and returned to the dressing room.

"The dress will be ready next week."

Just in time for the wedding. "I need shoes and a veil."

I browsed the store, finding a pair of comfortable sandals, and a veil that flowed over my hair and made a beautiful train behind me. I'd wear my mother's pearls when I walked down the aisle. Everything was ready.

My phone rang. Not recognizing the number, I almost didn't answer. "Hello?"

"It's Queen."

Chapter Twenty

I mouthed to Mom that Queen was on the phone. "Hello."

"Did you get my things?"

"You said you were going to call tomorrow." I strode to my car.

"I know, I know. Never mind that. So bring them to me tomorrow."

"I'm working, so it'll be after five."

"Whatever." She hung up.

Okay. I slid into the driver's seat. My phone immediately rang again. Mom this time. "Yes?"

"What did she want?"

"To know whether I had her things. I'll take them to her after work tomorrow, and yes, you can come. Shar has already insisted."

"Good. I'll be at the shop at five." Click.

People sure did seem in a hurry this evening. Not me. I'd enjoyed seeing how the wedding dress would look on me. I'd felt like Princess Diana with the cathedral veil, although mine wasn't nearly as long as hers. I grinned and turned toward the penthouse.

Brad met me at the door with a sub sandwich. "I figured you might be hungry." He gave me a tender kiss on my cheek.

"Starved." I plopped on the sofa, surrounded by my two cats and Sheba. "Queen called back. I'm to take her the things after work tomorrow." I bit into the Italian sub, the tangy taste of the sauce waking up my tastebuds. "Yummy."

Brad sat next to me, moving Sharkbait to his lap. "I'll worry, but I am glad one of the doll's eyes now holds a tracker. Plus, you've one on your phone. Keep it with you."

"I will. The department knows where Nellie lives." Now that I knew her real name, I'd use it rather than her pretentious nickname.

Brad stared off into the distance. "I've something to tell you."

My heart lurched. "What?"

"The Clarksons were found dead in their room. An aide went to fetch them when they didn't show up for supper. They were killed execution-style." His gaze returned to me.

I swallowed against a dry throat and set my sandwich on the coffee table. Sheba immediately wolfed it down in two bites. "It wouldn't have been Nellie. She didn't get along with her parents, but she wouldn't kill them."

"Hope you're right. McIlroy is about to call off your trip over there. I'm tending to agree with him."

"Too late now. I want to know why she wants that doll and painting." Appetite gone, I didn't care that my dog ate my supper. Instead, I went to bed, praying Nellie wasn't luring me into a trap.

The next morning after a quick breakfast of eggs and bacon with Brad, I took Sheba to open the store. I fed and watered the boarded animals, then let the dogs into the grassy enclosure to play before returning to my desk and booting up my computer.

Shar breezed in the front door. "Your mom said we're going to Queen's tonight."

"I'm not calling her that anymore. She's Nellie." The doll and painting waited in the back of the car for this afternoon. I was as ready as I could be to face Nellie again.

Brad brought the morning coffee, Heather shuffled in after a night sitting up with Robby who had a stomachache, and Mom popped in on her way to work. A normal morning in my world.

Did Nellie know about her parents yet? I couldn't find anything online about the murders, so I doubted it. It wasn't like McIlroy would call her. Not when he suspected her. I didn't want to be the one to tell her.

"Don't worry." Shar sent me a smile. "It'll work out. Always does."

Nodding, I turned back to my computer to pay some bills. Once, I'd thought I needed to be a veterinarian to be happy. Then, Brad had come along, disrupting my plans when he'd said he was going to raise the rent on all the shops in the mall. Instead, he met the people and decided to rebuild and renovate, making me fall in love. He'd guided me into making my doggy daycare and pet shop a success. Yes, things were working out. At least they were for me, so far. I would not worry about tonight.

At the end of the day, I collected the garbage and took it to the dumpster in the alley. I tossed the bag over the lip and turned, staring right into the barrel of a gun. My eyes traveled up a muscular arm and into the face of Willie. The man was covered head to toe in black clothes.

"Here's what we're going to do," he said. "We're going to get in your car and drive to see Queen."

"What makes you think I have them in my car?"

"Because the stupid woman told me." He grinned without humor. "She trusts me, you see. Now, let's go before one of your friends come out and I have to shoot them."

I yanked open the driver's-side door and climbed in as he moved to the passenger side. I clicked on my seatbelt, my brain whirling to find a way out of this predicament. My mind a blank. "Why the double cross?"

"No talking. Just drive. I'm not into that whole 'spill your guts' thing."

Drat. I'd left my cell phone on my desk. At least the doll sat in the back, and everyone knew where I planned on going. I glanced at my watch. Mom would be showing up any minute now.

"No dawdling. Push the limit. I want behind those locked gates before they discover you're missing."

"Hostage situation, huh?" When he didn't reply, I figured he was the only one allowed to talk. I drove the twenty minutes in silence.

When we arrived, Willie pulled a cell phone

CYNTHIA HICKEY

from his pocket and punched in a code. The iron
gates swung open, closing behind us. Well, I'd
wanted in; just didn't figure it would be this way.

"Don't try anything. Take the things out of the
back and climb those steps. Queen will figure out
I'm not here to do good soon enough."

"Her name is Nellie." Head high, I collected the
items and marched toward the front door.

It swung open before I could ring the bell.
Nellie's eyes narrowed. "You?"

"Step aside." Willie shoved me forward.

I stumbled over the entryway but righted myself
before I could fall. "Sorry. He grabbed me in back
of the shop."

"Of all my people, I didn't suspect you." Nellie
backed up.

"I was the perfect little servant. Into the living
room." He motioned with the gun. "Set those things
on the table."

I quickly complied, sitting on a white leather
sofa as soft as butter. It would be a shame for him to
shoot us and ruin the lovely piece of furniture.

"Now, tell me what is so important about these
things?" Willie sat across from us in a chair that
matched the sofa.

"There's a map inside the head. The other half is
in the painting." Nellie crossed her arms. "I don't
know if it leads to treasure. It's a story I've heard
my whole life. One of murder and intrigue and gold
coins." She laughed. "I don't have a lot of
challenges in my life anymore and thought
following the map might be fun. Who knows?
Maybe the stories are true."

Willie picked up the doll and smashed it against the table. The replacement eye with the tracker rolled across the table and onto the floor.

I quickly picked it up and dropped it into my pocket. Willie was too engrossed on the slip of paper that fell out of the doll to notice, but Nellie did.

Spots of crimson dotted her cheeks. She'd figured out I'd been there to lead the authorities to her. Luckily, her lips pressed together in a narrow line. Right on cue, sirens wailed in the distance.

Ignoring the sound, Willie removed the painting from its frame. "There's nothing here."

"Yes, there is. Follow me." Nellie took the painting to the kitchen and held it under the faucet. "The paint will wash off. I found the map as a kid, not knowing exactly what it was; just that I had something to paint on. It wasn't until I saw something online about vintage dolls and their hollow heads that I put the two together. Sounds untrue, doesn't it? That only makes it more fun. The tunnel under your house, Trinity, leads to another secret door. One I've never found in all the times I've played down there."

Fun for her, maybe, but what kind of child enjoys playing in dark tunnels? What would Willie do if there was no treasure? I glanced out the window. Red and blue lights flashed through the bars of the fence. "Can they get in?"

"Eventually," Nellie said. "All they have to do is find out what security company I use and get the info from them."

"A woman with your reputation would have

another way out." Willie aimed his gun at her head. "Am I right?"

Nellie nodded and huffed. "I didn't reach this point by being stupid." She led the way into the pantry and removed a throw rug to reveal a trapdoor. "Grab a flashlight from the shelf."

I took one and tossed another to her. Nice and heavy in my hand.

"Go." Willie poked me in the back with his weapon.

I took a deep breath and descended into darkness, Nellie right behind me. At the bottom of the ladder, I switched on my light. A tunnel very much like the one under my house stretched in front of me. "Where does it come out?"

"Behind the juniper bushes outside the gate. It's not as long as the one under your house. I keep a car there." Nellie stepped in front of me. "'For such a time as this,' as they say."

We moved through the narrow tunnel to another trapdoor. Nellie pushed it open and climbed out.

Very clever. Just enough sod covered the door to make it look like a permanent part of the yard. I shoved a branch out of my way and stepped out. Through the branches flickered the lights on the squad cars.

"Make a sound and you're dead." Willie aimed the gun at my head to prove his point.

I clamped my lips together. The tracker in my pocket was all the help I needed.

Nellie led us to an SUV parked between her house and a neighbor's. Seconds later, we were speeding out of town and into the country.

"The place is looking nice." Nellie peered through the front windshield.

"My fiancé has worked hard and spent a lot of money. We're getting married in a little over a week and will be living here." I shoved open my door.

"Don't count on it," Willie said, laughing. "I doubt the two of you will make it out of here alive."

"Then why help you?" I shined the light in his face.

"Because there's always a chance while you draw breath." He slapped the flashlight out of my hand. "There is no chance if you're dead."

I picked up the flashlight, wishing he'd turn around so I could slam it against his thick skull. He was right. As long as I breathed, I had a chance.

Chapter Twenty-one

"I can't believe you were going to betray me," Nellie hissed.

"Why haven't you alerted him?" I jerked my head over my shoulder.

"Because he'd shoot us both."

"Shut up." Willie tapped my head with the barrel of the gun. "No collaborating."

"Didn't know you knew such big words." Nellie's eyes glittered in the beam of my light.

"I'm going to enjoy getting rid of you."

I couldn't help but wonder what would happen to her fortune when she died. Years of accumulated wealth. Maybe it would go to pay back some of her victims.

"I really need to know who killed Jennings." If I was going to die, I wanted answers.

"Fine. I killed him," Willie said. "Bill and Ted were stealing for Queen. Jennings found out and snatched a pair of earrings from them. Said he was going to the police. I couldn't let that happen."

"But you weren't at the wedding."

"Yes, I was. Once the food was carried inside, I stayed outside most of the time. It wasn't hard to stab the man while everyone was focused on the wedding toasts. Satisfied?"

"No." Nellie wrapped her arms around her chest. "Why the double cross? I pay you well."

"I'm tired of being at your beck and call. Time to build my own empire."

It's always about money. My shoulders slumped. I had no bargaining power here, and I doubted he'd listen to anything Nellie said. Not that she'd help me after finding out I was going to turn her over to the police.

"Trinity!" Brad's voice came from behind us.

"Run." Willie gave me a shove and fired behind us.

"Stay back," I called out. Please, stay back. I'd find a way to survive this and marry Brad in my mother's dress.

"I said, run!" Willie gave me a push.

"Stop shoving me. I understand English." I sprinted after Nellie, colliding with her when she stopped suddenly.

"The secret door is around here somewhere."

If it exists. I shined my light on the walls.

Willie wavered between us and the tunnel behind us.

Roots and rocks littered the dirt walls. I studied one rock in particular, round and smooth—a perfect fit for a hand. I put mine over it and pushed.

A section of the wall opened. Bingo.

We stepped inside, the wall swinging back into place. The room was more of a cave. Water dripped down the wall.

"Where's the treasure?" Willie aimed his weapon at Nellie again.

"Look for it yourself."

"You don't give the orders anymore."

Good grief. Let the two bicker. I shined my light around the space. A treasure put here a long time ago might not be easy to see. "Who supposedly hid something here?" The thick walls muffled my voice.

"My grandfather." Nellie chuckled. "We've been thieves for generations. Story goes that his father robbed a stagecoach, and that's where the coins came from. My father always denied it, though. That's why I kept visiting my parents. To find out if the story was true. When he insisted I let it be, I knew there was something to the story."

"Your parents are dead. I'm sorry." I gestured with my head at Willie. "My guess is that he did it."

She whirled. "Did you?"

"Yep. No loose ends."

If this room was to be my grave, I wouldn't look for the coins anymore. Why help an evil man get rich?

Brad and McIlroy would never find our bodies. Tears pricked my eyes. I started to slide to the floor when I realized Willie's full attention was on Nellie.

I slid across the back wall, trying to move behind him. I clutched my flashlight like a sword. Bashing him in the head would give me a lot of satisfaction, even if he turned and shot me. At least I'd get one good lick in.

"They had nothing to do with any of this. My father stopped his life of crime years ago. They were innocent." Nellie's hands curled into fists.

"You deserve the same death." He pressed the trigger.

Nellie's eyes opened wide, then she fell.

Without thinking, I lunged and whacked Willie. He fell to his knees. I wasn't waiting around but pressed the rock and darted into the tunnel, closing the door behind me, then raced back the way we'd come.

It didn't take long before the pounding of feet alerted me that Willie was close behind. I shut off the flashlight and felt my way. Complete darkness surrounded me. If I couldn't see, then neither could he.

"I'm going to kill you slowly and enjoy every second." His voice, deep and gravelly, sent spiders scurrying down my spine. I'd hoped to run into McIlroy and the other officers coming my way, and realized they probably went to the end of the tunnel thinking we'd come out there.

I hurried as fast as I could. When I reached the stairs, I fell forward, bashing my shins. Pain radiated up my legs. I crawled to the top and shoved open the door, slamming it behind me. We hadn't replaced the broken lock yet. I scurried from under the stairs in search of something with which to jam the door.

Cursing came from inside the closet. Forget jamming the door. Get out of the house.

I dashed through the open front door, seeking a place to hide. Rather than dart across an open meadow, I dashed into the woods, still clutching the flashlight I didn't dare turn on.

The moon played peek-a-boo with the clouds providing me with some light. I stayed in the shadows as best I could. Finding a thick pile of brush, I peered out for any sign of Willie. Was Nellie dead? I hoped not, despite her crimes, I kind of liked her.

Willie stood in the middle of the yard, staring at the two squad cars and Brad's Mercedes. He removed something from his pocket. When he started slashing tires, I realized he'd pulled a knife. Smart. A gun would alert the police to his whereabouts. Finished, he straightened. "Come on out. It's only a matter of time before I find you."

I clamped a hand over my mouth, certain he could hear me breathing. Please think I've headed for the road.

No such luck. He headed for the trees.

Moving as quietly as possible, I stayed perpendicular to the meadow, knowing the police would be at the other end where we'd found Nellie's brother. All I had to do was make it there alive.

I whirled and choked off a shriek as something crashed through the brush, then sagged with relief to see Sheba. "Oh, girl," I whispered. "You're a welcome sight." I gave her a quick hug, no longer feeling alone.

More crashing, this time from behind, spurred me forward. The shack, although still far away, came into view as the clouds parted. Should I risk the shortcut across the meadow? Willie didn't seem to want to fire his weapon. I decided to chance it and left the safety of the trees.

Crouching down, I raced across the open field, Sheba by my side. Spotting Brad, I waved my arms. "Brad!"

He whipped around and raced toward me, wrapping me in his arms. "I've never been so scared."

"We can't stand here. He's coming." I tugged him to where the other officers stood. "There."

McIlroy, Snowe, and Rice pulled their weapons and faced the field. The man would be hard to see in his dark clothes.

Brad and I stood in the protection of the building. The police could take it from there.

"He shot Nellie. She's in a secret room in the tunnel. We need to find out if she's still alive."

"We will." He kept his arm around me. "After the police take care of Willy."

"Police. Drop your weapon." McIlroy raised his gun.

Willie fired.

All three of law enforcement opened fired. Seconds later, all was quiet.

"You okay?" McIlroy glanced my way.

"Yes, but Nellie might be dying under the house."

He nodded, then turned to the other officers. "Handle this. I'll meet up with you later."

We squeezed into the front of Brad's new, old truck and bounced our way back to the house. McIlroy's eyes slitted as he spotted the slashed tires.

"Come on. Worry about that later." I rushed them into the house as McIlroy called for an ambulance.

Minutes later, we stood over Nellie. McIlroy checked for a pulse. "She's alive." He shined a penlight on the wound in her side. "A couple of inches to the left and she'd have been gut shot."

"I'll wait upstairs for the ambulance." Relief flooded through me. Nellie would spend a long time in jail, but at least she wasn't dead.

Fifteen minutes later, an ambulance roared to a stop in front of the house. It wouldn't be easy squeezing a stretcher through the closet and into the tunnel.

I sat on the top step as Brad joined me. "What a crazy few weeks this has been."

He took my hand. "Pretty much the norm." The corner of his mouth twitched.

"If anything bad happens at our wedding, I'm going to throw a fit."

"Our wedding will be perfect. Just like you. What could go wrong?"

Chapter Twenty-two

My hands shook as I tried to apply a soft pink lipstick to my lips. After the third smear, I gave up.

"Let me." Heather took the lipstick and quickly applied it to my lips. "You're a beautiful bride. Good choice wearing your mother's wedding dress. It's perfect."

"Oh." Mom entered the tent where my dressing room was located and immediately started crying. "Now, I've gone and ruined my makeup, but you look so gorgeous. Even better than I did on my wedding day."

"I doubt that." I smiled, although I felt like royalty. Why had I been so stubborn about holding onto my independence for so long? Brad didn't stifle me. He expressed his concerns, warned me once in a while, but always supported my decision no matter how dangerous he thought it to be. What a ninny I'd been.

"Is your house ready?" Shar asked, handing Mom my veil.

"The master bedroom and bath, and the kitchen are fully renovated. Workers will continue on the rest of the house during the work week." I laughed. "We've put a new lock on the door to the tunnel. I've already blocked it with boxes of Christmas decorations." I had no desire to go down there again.

"Hello, ladies." Dad stood in the doorway, a photograph in his hand. "Want to know what the authorities found in the room where Nellie was shot?" He handed me the picture.

I glanced down at a box of gold coins. "Oh, my. Are they real?"

"Sure as shootin'."

"What happens to them now?"

"They're yours."

I blinked like an owl. "Mine?"

"Found on your property. Worth quite a bundle, if I do say so myself. McIlroy has them locked up at the station until you're ready to retrieve them."

I fell onto a padded chair. Mine and Brad's. What in the world? We didn't need that much money. Brad already had more than we'd ever spend. I glanced at my friends and family knowing exactly what I'd ask Brad to do with them.

"Ready?" Dad crooked his arm. "You look so much like your mother did on our wedding day that it gets me right here." He put a hand over his heart.

"You sure you want the dogs involved?" Shar glanced at Sheba who wore a flowered collar, and Barney whose collar held a tiny box with the wedding rings.

"Of course. They'll be wonderful." I linked my arm with my father's. I couldn't get married without my fur babies.

Mom headed to her seat in the front row as the dogs, then Shar, then Heather lined up in front of Dad and me on the white carpet runner. I took a deep breath as the music started and prepared to take that first step that would lead me to Brad.

My hands started shaking again. Dad put his calming one over mine. "Don't fret. I couldn't wish for a better man for my daughter."

Tears welled. "He is the best." Caring, brave, and smart. I was a lucky woman.

We moved to the arch next to the water where Dad placed my hand in Brad's.

"Wow," Brad whispered.

My face heated. He looked pretty darn good, too. More handsome than was legal in his tuxedo.

As the sun started to set, the preacher began, "Dearly Beloved…"

The rest of the ceremony passed in a blur as I lost myself in Brad's gaze only jerking out of my trance when my husband lifted my veil to kiss me. We'd done it.

We headed down the makeshift aisle as wedding guests blew bubbles. In the limousine, I turned to Brad. "I'd like to divide the gold coins among my parents, Heather, and Shar. We don't need them, and I might not have even been here without those four."

Brad squeezed my hand. "That's a great idea. They get you into trouble, but they also help get you out." He pulled me close for a kiss. "I love your heart, Trinity Armstrong."

I smiled and nestled in his arms. Yes, I was a lucky woman.

The End

Dear Reader,

Sometimes, real life is as crazy as fiction. The snake on the boat really happened during a camping trip we took, except it was with friends and not my parents. We were with a ninety-one-year-old and an eighty-four-year-old. The younger one sees only shadows without a huge magnifying glass so was absolutely terrified. So was I. I hate snakes and spiders. My brave hubby is the one who battled the snake, and our dog is a Corgi, not a Mastiff. But, I had to put this crazy adventure in a book. Hope you enjoyed it.

As for the doll and the painting, they were in our house when we bought it. Kind of creepy to go into a room and see a Victorian porcelain doll hanging from her neck. Of course, nothing else was sinister in the house, but the family has had great fun hiding it in places to startle each other. We've even stuffed it in our son's backpack when he boarded a plane for a nice surprise when he reached his home, and we've shipped it across country.

I hope you've enjoyed *Wedding Day Cat Burglar*. If so, please visit Amazon and leave a review. Reviews are important to an author.

God Bless,

Cynthia

WEDDING DAY CAT BURGLAR

If you're enjoying the Tail Waggin' series, you might enjoy my Tiny House series. Enjoy the first chapter of No Small Caper.

Chapter One

"It's your job now to keep these crazies in line, Miss Turley." Lenora Rice of Heavenly Acres dropped a heavy key ring into my outstretched hand. Her gaze raked over me. "You don't look big enough for this job."

"Call me CJ." Excitement over my new position and beautiful home bubbled up like an Arkansas hot spring. I set down Caper, the spaniel-mix puppy I'd inherited and let her explore.

"I don't need to call you anything. I'm outta here. Good luck." The woman scrunched up her nose and turned away.

"Wait. Can't you give me some pointers? What do you mean by crazies?"

"Oh." She handed me a folder. "Here are the lists of renters and homeowners. Crazies? Like a bunch of twisted trees. You'll meet all kinds. It's up to you to monitor the grounds, see to repairs, collect rent and lot fees, etc. You're like…a leasing agent. Yeah, like that. Good chance you'll never see the owner. He's a recluse. Make friends with the man in house number seven. Name is Eric Drake. He's a park ranger and knows all there is to know about the area. There's food in the fridge—not a lot, just the essentials—until you make it to the store. No cars in the community. Everyone has other means of transportation from the parking lot to their home. It's a quiet place… most of the time."

I glanced at the concrete path that circled the lake. "That's it?"

"Yep. Might as well get settled and start meeting the kooks. Oh, and there's been a rash of robberies. Might want to look into that." She spun around, rushed to an older model sedan and sped away, leaving me standing with boxes piled around my feet. I heaved a sigh and regarded the green and white house the size of my parents' bedroom that sat on wheels.

The fifth key I tried unlocked the door to my new home. I stepped into a bright and airy room painted white with green trim to match the exterior. A forest-green love seat sat across from an entertainment center that housed a small television with room for my books, thank goodness. A counter ran along one wall with a single sink and a two-burner stove. Under the counter were nestled a washer/dryer combo, a tiny fridge, and cupboards. A small door led to a walk-in shower and compost toilet. Stairs with drawers inserted into each step led to a loft where a queen-size memory-foam mattress took up most of the space. I could just stand in the center of my "bedroom."

On each side of the bed were closets and drawers that extended from floor to ceiling. My tiny home had everything I needed. With a happy sigh, I headed outside to drag in my boxes. Soon I realized how small my space was as I struggled to find a place for everything, but somehow I managed. A bookshelf and pretty storage boxes at the foot of my bed would help, so I made a note to purchase those as soon as possible. Until then, I piled the boxes on their sides and used them in place of a bookcase.

I grabbed a protein bar from the food items I'd thought to bring, shut Caper up in the house since I couldn't trust the little scamp not to get into trouble, and headed to a fairly new golf cart with bright red seats.

The key hung in the ignition. Strange thing to do if robbers were milling around. Still, with a couple of hours of daylight left, I decided to drive through the community. I could meet those out and about, and the rest could wait until the next day. I clapped my hands, eager to get started, then headed down the path.

Trees lined my way with colorful homes appearing now and again. To my left, Lake Blue Waters, aptly named, sparkled in the late afternoon sun. Already peace started to erase the stress caused from taking care of a dying grandmother. I'd quit a job as a 911 operator to care for Gammy and when she died, I wanted something more…relaxing. When I'd spotted the ad in the paper for overseer of Heavenly Acres, I jumped at the opportunity.

"Hello." I stopped the cart in front of a home the color of bananas with purple gingerbread trim. An elderly woman wearing the largest floppy hat I'd ever seen straightened from her bed of peonies. "I'm CJ Turley, the new overseer."

"I'm Mrs. Snyder, you can call me Mags." She pushed her hat off her face and narrowed her eyes. "How old are you?"

"Twenty-six. Why?" Strange question when you first meet someone.

"I can see you're going to need my help. Why they hired a child is beyond me. I'm sure you're aware we have a thief?"

"I've heard as much." I grinned. "I'm happy for all the help I can get. Has anyone called the police?"

"That handsome park ranger is responsible for this community, for the most part. Good thing, because the local police department, which has all of three officers, isn't worth squat. Come in and have a cup of tea." She turned without waiting for an answer and disappeared into her home.

Shrugging, I turned off the cart, pocketed the key,

and followed her into a house so reminiscent of my grandmother's it brought tears to my eyes. Doilies and afghans covered every available surface. Family portraits filled the walls. She'd managed to cram so many treasures into the place it left little room to walk. A calico cat blinked up at me from the sofa. "Hello, gorgeous."

The cat hissed and darted to the loft only to appear on a ledge that circled the home. She peered down at me with big green eyes.

"Callie isn't friendly to strangers, but she won't bite." Mrs. Snyder fetched two mismatched tea cups, filled them, and handed one to me. "There's sugar and cream on the coffee table."

One sniff of the tea, mint green, and I knew I didn't need anything added. "Cute home."

"Too much stuff, but at my age, you don't want to get rid of anything. I've lost a set of emerald earrings to that robbing scoundrel, so I'm relying on you to find them." She slid sideways into a rocking chair across from me.

"What about the ranger?"

"Eric's working on it." She sipped her drink. "He's a busy man, so don't go bothering him."

Yes, ma'am. "Can you tell me about the other residents?"

"Houses one through seven are owners, the rest renters and I think only ten, eleven, and twelve are occupied right now. You're in number one, of course. There's a young married couple in two that stay to themselves. Newlyweds." She chuckled. "A middle-aged widower in three, a single harlot in four, a single mom in six, I'm in five, but you know that. It's suppertime, so don't go knocking on any doors. Wait until morning."

Bossy woman, but I could tell we would be great friends. "I'm just getting acquainted with the area tonight."

"Good. You have a head on your shoulders." She stood and removed the cup from my hand. "My shows are on. See you tomorrow. I'm here to help."

My eyes widened. "Of course."

She rushed me outside.

Laughing, I resumed my ride around the lake, pleased with how orderly and kept up the yards were. The "harlot" in four was the only house that needed improvement. Weeds grew up around the tires of her red and white house, a few shingles looked loose, nothing that couldn't be fixed. I'd approach the subject with her when I introduced myself.

Slowing down, I approached number seven, hoping to catch a glimpse of the handsome park ranger. The door opened, and he didn't disappoint. A man who had to stand over six feet in his socks with hair the color of milk chocolate and eyes the color of coffee stepped onto a postage-sized porch. He leaned on the wood railing.

"Good afternoon."

"Good afternoon." I stopped. "I'm CJ Turley, the new overseer."

"Eric Drake, ranger." A dimple winked in his cheek. "You're a lot prettier than Ms. Rice."

My face flushed, and I patted my almost black hair, pleased I'd let it hang loose around my shoulders. I'd spent so much time caring for Grams the last five years, good-looking men were foreign to me, unless they were over the age of sixty. "Uh, thanks."

"Where you headed?"

"Just getting familiar with the area."

He hopped off the porch, wearing flip-flops on his feet, and climbed into the cart. "Then I'm the best guide you'll get. Have you met anyone else?"

"Mrs. Snyder." My hands trembled as I steered back onto the path.

"Crusty, lovable soul." He placed his arm along the seat back. "I guess she told you about the other owners?"

I nodded, my mouth drying up as his fingers brushed my shoulder. He moved, and I sighed, silly enough to hope he'd put them back. "Anything I need to know about my job?"

"Do you know how to fix things?"

I grinned. "I do. My father treated me like a son. I can even rebuild engines, with the proper tools."

"You sure don't look like a boy." He leaned over and peered at my face. "Grey eyes. I'd wondered."

There went the dreaded flush again. Experience had taught me that my face was as red as a berry. I cleared my throat. "You're a flirt."

"Guilty." He laughed, not seeming in the least bit embarrassed. "You're a welcome sight, CJ."

"I'm sure you see lots of sights in the forest."

"Animals, not pretty girls. Stop right here. You don't want to miss this."

I obeyed. "Oh." The setting sun kissed the lake with gold. Yes, I was going to like Heavenly Acres. Movement in the bushes to my right drew my attention.

A teenage boy jumped up, a red laptop under his arm, and darted away.

"Hey." I leaped from the cart and gave chase. A yapping behind me alerted me to the fact Caper had escaped the house, unless... "That's my laptop." Would we catch the thief on the first day?

"Hold back." Eric, now barefoot, bolted past me.

The boy dropped the laptop in a bush and dove into the lake. Eric splashed after him but gave up and trudged back dripping. "I guess we know who the thief is."

I retrieved my laptop and dog, putting both in the golf cart. "I'll have all the locks on the houses changed tomorrow." I stared after the swimming culprit. "Have you seen him before?"

"No, but my guess is he came from the campgrounds across from us. I'll ask around in the morning." He swept Caper into his arms and climbed back in the cart, keeping my pup in his lap. Lucky girl. "Cute dog."

"She's a rascal. I inherited her when Gammy died." I ruffled the dog's head. That boy could have caused her to be lost, and despite the trouble she caused more often than not, I enjoyed her company. I stared across the lake. Eric wouldn't be the only one asking questions the next day.

Website at www.cynthiahickey.com

www.cynthiahickey.com
Multi-published and best-selling author, Cynthia Hickey, has taught writing at many conferences and small writing retreats. She and her husband run the publishing press, Winged Publications, which includes some of the CBA's best well-known authors. They live in Arizona and Arkansas, becoming snowbirds with two dogs and one cat. They have ten grandchildren who them busy and tell everyone they know that "Nana is a writer."

Connect with me on FaceBook
Twitter
Sign up for my newsletter and receive a free short story
www.cynthiahickey.com

Follow me on Amazon
And Bookbub

Enjoy other books by Cynthia Hickey

The Tail Waggin' Mysteries
Cat-Eyed Witness
The Dog Who Found a Body
Troublesome Twosome
Four-Legged Suspect
Unwanted Christmas Guest

Tiny House Mysteries

No Small Caper
Caper Goes Missing
Caper Finds a Clue
Caper's Dark Adventure
A Strange Game for Caper
Caper Steals Christmas
Caper Finds a Treasure
Tiny House Mysteries boxed set

A Hollywood Murder
Killer Pose, book 1
Killer Snapshot, book 2
Shoot to Kill, book 3
Kodak Kill Shot, book 4
To Snap a Killer
Hollywood Murder Mysteries

Shady Acres Mysteries
Beware the Orchids, book 1
Path to Nowhere
Poison Foliage
Poinsettia Madness
Deadly Greenhouse Gases
Vine Entrapment
Shady Acres Boxed Set

Wife for Hire – Private Investigators
Saving Sarah
Lesson for Lacey
Mission for Meghan
Long Way for Lainie
Aimed at Amy
Wife for Hire (all five in one)

Brothers Steele
Sharp as Steele

Carved in Steele
Forged in Steele
Brothers Steele (All three in one)

The Brothers of Copper Pass
Wyatt's Warrant
Dirk's Defense
Stetson's Secret
Houston's Hope
Dallas's Dare
Seth's Sacrifice
Malcolm's Misunderstanding
The Brothers of Copper Pass Boxed Set

Time Travel
The Portal

CLEAN BUT GRITTY Romantic Suspense

Highland Springs

Murder Live
Say Bye to Mommy
To Breathe Again
Highland Springs Murders (all 3 in one)

Colors of Evil Series

Shades of Crimson
Coral Shadows

The Pretty Must Die Series

Ripped in Red, book 1

Pierced in Pink, book 2
Wounded in White, book 3
Worthy, The Complete Story

Lisa Paxton Mystery Series

Eenie Meenie Miny Mo
Jack Be Nimble
Hickory Dickory Dock
Boxed Set

Secrets of Misty Hollow

Hearts of Courage
A Heart of Valor
The Game
Suspicious Minds
After the Storm
Local Betrayal
Hearts of Courage Boxed Set

Overcoming Evil series
Mistaken Assassin
Captured Innocence
Mountain of Fear
Exposure at Sea
A Secret to Die for
Collision Course
Romantic Suspense of 5 books in 1

INSPIRATIONAL

Nosy Neighbor Series
Anything For A Mystery, Book 1
A Killer Plot, Book 2

Skin Care Can Be Murder, Book 3
Death By Baking, Book 4
Jogging Is Bad For Your Health, Book 5
Poison Bubbles, Book 6
A Good Party Can Kill You, Book 7
Nosy Neighbor collection

Christmas with Stormi Nelson

The Summer Meadows Series
Fudge-Laced Felonies, Book 1
Candy-Coated Secrets, Book 2
Chocolate-Covered Crime, Book 3
Maui Macadamia Madness, Book 4
All four novels in one collection

The River Valley Mystery Series
Deadly Neighbors, Book 1
Advance Notice, Book 2
The Librarian's Last Chapter, Book 3
All three novels in one collection

Historical cozy
Hazel's Quest

Historical Romances
Runaway Sue
Taming the Sheriff
Sweet Apple Blossom
A Doctor's Agreement
A Lady Maid's Honor
A Touch of Sugar
Love Over Par
Heart of the Emerald

A Sketch of Gold
Her Lonely Heart

Finding Love the Harvey Girl Way
Cooking With Love
Guiding With Love
Serving With Love
Warring With Love
All 4 in 1

Finding Love in Disaster
The Rancher's Dilemma
The Teacher's Rescue
The Soldier's Redemption

Woman of courage Series

A Love For Delicious
Ruth's Redemption
Charity's Gold Rush
Mountain Redemption
They Call Her Mrs. Sheriff
Woman of Courage series

Short Story Westerns
Desert Rose
Desert Lilly
Desert Belle
Desert Daisy
Flowers of the Desert 4 in 1

Contemporary

Romance in Paradise
Maui Magic

Sunset Kisses
Deep Sea Love
3 in 1

Finding a Way Home
Service of Love
Hillbilly Cinderella
Unraveling Love
I'd Rather Kiss My Horse

Christmas
Dear Jillian
Romancing the Fabulous Cooper Brothers
Handcarved Christmas
The Payback Bride
Curtain Calls and Christmas Wishes
Christmas Gold
A Christmas Stamp
Snowflake Kisses
Merry's Secret Santa
A Christmas Deception

The Red Hat's Club (Contemporary novellas)

Finally
Suddenly
Surprisingly
The Red Hat's Club 3 – in 1

Short Story

One Hour (A short story thriller)
Whisper Sweet Nothings (a Valentine short romance)

Made in United States
North Haven, CT
27 July 2023

39582427R00117